A King Production presents…

Bad Bitches Only

ASSASSINS…

EPISODE 1
(Be Careful With Me)

JOY DEJA KING

Cover concept by Joy Deja King
Cover model: Joy Deja King

Library of Congress Cataloging-in-Publication Data;
A King Production
Assassins...Bad Bitches Only Episode 1/by Joy Deja King

For complete Library of Congress Copyright info visit;
www.joydejaking.com
Twitter @joydejaking

A King Production
P.O. Box 912, Collierville, TN 38027

A King Production and the above portrayal log are trademarks of A King Production LLC

This Book is Dedicated To My:

Family, Readers and Supporters.
I LOVE you guys so much. Please believe that!!

--Joy Deja King

"Be Careful With Me
Yeah, It's Not A Threat, It's A Warnin'
Be Careful With Me
Yeah, My Heart Is Like A Package
With A Fragile Label On It
Be Careful With Me..."

~Cardi B~

A KING PRODUCTION

Bad Bitches Only

ASSASSINS...

EPISODE 1

(Be Careful With Me)

JOY DEJA KING

Chapter One

HE LOVES ME

Bailey strutted out the Hartsfield-Jackson Atlanta International Airport, in her strappy, four inch snakeskin shoes, wearing matte black wire frame square sunglas ses and a designer suit tailored to fit her size six frame perfectly. The brown beauty looked like she was a partner at a powerful law firm, when actually she was barely a second year law student. But school was the least of her worries. Bailey had other things on her mind, like the promise ring she was wearing. It cost more than some people's home. Don't get it confused, this wasn't a promise of sexual abstinence. This was a promise of marriage, from her boyfriend of five years, Dino Jacobs.

"Keera," I was just about to call you girl," Bailey said, getting in her car.

"I was shocked as shit when you answered. I was expecting to leave a voicemail. You said you was gonna be in some conferences all day," Keera replied.

"Girl, I was but I checked out early. I'm back in the A."

"You back in Atlanta?!" Keera questioned, sounding surprised.

"Yep. That's why I was calling you. So we could do drinks later on tonight at that spot we like." Baily was getting hyped, as she was dropping the top on her Lunar Blue Metallic E 400 Benz.

"Most definitely...so where you headed now."

"Where you think...home to my man! Stop playin'," Bailey laughed, getting on interstate 75.

"I know yo' boo, will be happy to see you."

"Yep and his ass gon' be surprised too. He thinks I'm coming back tomorrow night. But I missed my baby. Plus that conference was boring as hell. All them snobby ass lawyers was workin' my nerves."

"Get used to it, cause you about to be one," Keera reminded her.

"Yeah but only cause Dino insisted. You know

I wanted to attend beauty school. I love all things hair and makeup. I have zero interest in law. But that nigga the one paying for it, so it's whatever," Bailey smacked.

"Girl, don't be wasting that man money. You better get yo' law degree and handle them cases!" Keera giggled.

"Okaaaay!! I believe Dino just want me to be able to represent his ass, in case anything go down," Bailey snickered.

"Well, let me get off the phone so you can get home."

"Keera, I know how to talk and drive at the same damn time," she popped.

"I didn't say you didn't but umm I have a nail appointment. You know they be swamped on a Friday," Keera explained.

"True. Okay, go get yo' raggedy nails done," Bailey joked. "Call me later, so we can decide what time we meeting for drinks."

"Will do! Talk to you later on."

When Bailey got off the phone with Keera, she immediately started blasting some Cardi B. The music, mixed with the nice summer breeze blowing through her hair, had her feeling sexy. She began imagining the dick down she'd get from Dino, soon as she got home.

"Here I come baby," Bailey smiled, pulling in the driveway. She was practically skipping inside the house and up the stairs, giddy like a silly schoolgirl. You'd think hearing Silk's old school Freak Me, echoing down the hallway, in the middle of the afternoon, would've sent the alarm ringing in Bailey's head. Instead, it made her try to reach her man faster.

It wasn't until she got a few steps from the slightly ajar bedroom door, did her heart start racing. Next came the rapid breathing and finally came dread. You know the type of dread, that seems like it's worse than death but you don't know for sure because you've never actually died. It was all too much for Bailey. Her eyes were bleeding blood. She wanted to erase everything she just witnessed and rewind time.

I shoulda kept my ass in DC, she screamed to herself, heading back downstairs and leaving the house. Once outside, Bailey started to vomit in the bushes, until there was nothing left in her stomach.

Chapter Two

PROPOSITION

"Who in the world is banging on the damn door," Shiffon huffed, tossing the television remote down. She looked out the peephole and saw her cousin. "Girl, why you knockin' so hard? The doorbell work just fine," she snapped, opening the screen door.

"You ain't gon' believe what just happened," Bailey fumed, still in shock. "Is Auntie Deb here?" she asked, putting her purse down.

"Nah, she still at work...why?" Shiffon closed the door, wondering what was up with her cousin.

"What about your little brother Milo?"

"Bailey, ain't nobody fuckin' here but me. What the hell is going on wit' you?" Shiffon barked.

"Girl, you ain't gon' believe what that fuckin' nigga Dino did!" Once Bailey knew they were alone, she got turnt up. "I come home early from that fuckin' bullshit conference, wanting to surprise my man wit' some pussy, and I see another bitch, riding my man's dick in the fuckin' bed I sleep in!"

"Is they dead?" Shiffon asked point blank.

"No." Bailey's voice went from crazed woman to saddened. "I walked out. They didn't even know I was there."

"You a better bitch than me." Shiffon shook her head, sitting down. She picked the remote back up, to unmute the show she was watching and continued eating her chips.

"So, you just gon' sit there and act like I ain't about to have a nervous breakdown," Bailey complained.

"You said you walked out. I assumed that meant, you good."

"Well I'm not!" Bailey exclaimed, picking up the remote and turning the television off. "Now, do I have your full attention."

Shiffon wasn't in the mood to listen to her cousin whine about Dino. She was dealing with her own bullshit but they had been close at one time, so she felt obligated to tolerate her venting.

"I'm listening." Shiffon shrugged.

"Dino was in bed Latoria." Bailey spoke in a flat tone.

"Obviously, you know the chick but you being so blasé." Shiffon gave a puzzled stare.

"Latoria...Tori, my best fuckin' friend!" Bailey screamed.

"How was I supposed to know Tori was short for Latoria? It ain't like I've ever met any of yo' friends before. But damn, that's fucked up!" Shiffon quipped. "Niggas ain't shit."

"You always used to say not to trust no bitch."

"And no nigga," Shiffon quickly added, cutting Bailey off.

True but come to find out my best fuckin' friend been gettin' dicked down by my man! That shit hurt." Bailey wanted to weep but was too angry.

"That's some cold and bold shit right there. How the fuck you just walk out. You didn't throw no shoes, lamp...nothing?" Shiffon sat there baffled.

"Traumatized, is the only way I can describe it. You know me Shiffon, so I ain't gonna sit on this couch and act like I didn't know Dino fucked around. When he be in them streets, handling business, the temptation is real."

Shiffon nodded her head in agreement. She knew all too well how shit went when your man was in the game. She didn't come out her relationship unscathed, and was still dealing with the after affects.

"But I always believed Dino respected me and what we shared," Bailey said, stoically.

"Why...cause of that promise ring on yo' finger?" Shiffon smacked.

Bailey glanced down at the diamond on her finger. She remembered the day Dino gave it to her. It was the fourth ring he had gotten her, each one more lavish then the last. But she should've gotten the hint after the third one, Dino had no intentions of making her his wife.

"I guess," Bailey admitted, fidgeting with her ring. "Then he was putting me through law school," she added.

"Nobody ever said Dino wasn't a smart nigga. When you out here selling drugs, it's a good idea to make sure yo' girl know the law inside and out," Shiffon reasoned. "I give him props for the innovative thinking."

"I bet them muthafuckas be lying in bed, laughing at my ass. Thinking I got to be the dumbest bitch ever." Bailey fussed. "I had lunch with Tori before I went out of town. She was cheesing all in my face like we besties, all while she couldn't wait for me to catch my flight, so she could play house wit' my nigga! I hate her and him!" Bailey picked up the throw pillow on the couch and kept punching it over and over again.

"Chile, why didn't you show that same energy when you caught those two clowns fuckin' in yo' bed. You ain't 'bout to fuck my mom's pillow up." Shiffon snatched it out of Bailey's hands.

"They gon' pay for this shit!" Bailey got a crazed gaze in her eyes.

"Sis, I love you but you know you ain't leaving Dino. You too addicted to that life. When the last time you even had a job?"

"You one to talk!" Bailey shot back. "Before Clay got locked up, you was living like a queen. Every time I saw you, you were driving a new whip, dripping in diamonds and dressed designer down."

"Yeah, and look at my ass now. I had to leave Philly and move back home wit' my mama. I ain't got shit," she scoffed.

"When the Feds locked Clay up, they raided our crib and took everything! All I've been doing is sittin' on this couch, tryna figure out how I'ma eat without begging my mom for a handout," Shiffon fumed, with resentment.

"What if I gave you a way out? I can help you get back on your feet."

"How? Based on what you just told me, you better be working on an exit plan for yo' damn self. You might come home and Dino got the locks changed and another bitch done moved in and took yo' place," Shiffon warned.

"Nah, that shit ain't gonna happen to me!" Bailey

spoke with defiance. "I have an idea that can get us both out of our fucked up predicament."

"Do tell," Shiffon said, munching on her chips.

"Dino has an apartment where he keeps a shit load of money and drugs. You can go there and take it."

"Why the fuck don't you just go there and take it?"

"Because Dino would know I did it, and he'd kill me."

"Like he wouldn't kill me too!" Shiffon popped.

"He wouldn't know it was you. I would get you a copy of the key, but you can make it look like someone broke in. You can do it when Dino and I are together, that way my whereabouts are accounted for. He'll never think I set the shit up."

"Girl, I don't know about this. Are you even sure Dino still uses the place to stash his shit?"

"He was still using it a couple months ago. He was out of town and one of his workers got himself in a situation and needed some money asap. Dino sent me to the spot to get the money for the guy."

"What if some people staying there now?"

"I highly doubt it," Bailey insisted. "The place wasn't even furnished. It might've had a couch or some shit. It's strictly a spot for money and drugs."

"I hear you." Shiffon exhaled and folded her arms. Bailey could tell her cousin was reluctant to be a part of her scheme.

"Ain't you tired of living like this? You ain't even got yo' own bedroom here. You sleeping on the fuckin' couch. Do you even know what your next move is gonna be?" she asked Shiffon.

Shiffon glanced down at her nails. She tried to maintain them herself but the polish was chipped. She had a head full of hair but was use to going to the beauty salon, getting sew-in weaves or custom wigs, so she never took the time to learn how to take care for her own natural hair. For now, Shiffon just kept it in a messy bun. Although her body was on point, it was hidden under basic gear. Shiffon would be lying to herself, if she pretended to be content with her current predicament.

"How much money we talkin' 'bout?" Shifffon wanted to know, while weighing the pros and the cons.

"I'm not sure but I think, I can give you at least twenty thousand and you can keep the drugs," Bailey added.

"I don't want them fuckin' drugs. I need cash."

"Alright but you gon' have to dump the shit or something because it ain't gonna look like a robbery if you leave the drugs.'"

"True. But I'ma need thirty thousand."

"I don't even know how much money you leaving wit'. It may not be that much," Bailey protested.

"Girl bye! I know you. If you offering twenty, then you can give me thirty, or you steal the shit yo'self," Shiffon countered.

"Fine! Seeing how pissed off Dino's gonna be, it's worth the extra ten g's."

"Bailey, you sure you wanna do this?"

"Positive. Once I get that money, I'm leaving that nigga. I'm done. I gave Dino my heart and he just shit on me wit' my own best friend," she said shaking her head.

"Okay, so you have a plan to get revenge on Dino, what about that chick?" Shiffon asked.

"Her ass is dust too but let me handle Dino first. I don't want to raise any suspicions. One thing law school has taught me, is to be a finisher and I'ma finish both of those muthafuckers off," Bailey promised.

Chapter Three

MURDER FOR HIRE

It had been well over a week since Bailey sat down on the couch across from her cousin and asked her to rob Dino. At first, Shiffon figured Bailey changed her mind but then she showed up with a key to his apartment. She wavered taking the it, until reminding herself, how dire her situation was and an easy robbery, could change all that. Once Shiffon decided to move forward, she asked Bailey to give her upfront money to cover expenses. She didn't want to go into this, with any surprises, so Shiffon had a plan of her own.

When Shiffon arrived at the apartment complex on Cheshire Bridge Rd, she parked the rental car across the street, before making her way inside the building. She was dressed professionally, carrying a briefcase and even wore some non-prescription reading glasses to compliment her attire. These items, including the rental car, were all purchased with the upfront cash Bailey gave her. Shiffon's initial trip to the apartment complex was to scope things out. She wanted a feel of her environment before making her money move. She also, needed to confirm the key Bailey gave her worked, before wasting anymore time.

Being cautious, Shiffon knocked on the door to make sure no one was inside. After waiting a minute or so with no answer, she reached into the briefcase to retrieve the key.

"Can I help you?"

Luckily Shiffon's head was down when she heard the door open, so the person standing in front of her, missed seeing the shocked look on her face. She was able to keep her cool, as Shiffon had prepared herself, for the small probability someone might be home.

"Good afternoon, I'm Dianne Miller and I work

for Farmers Insurance. This month we're having a special on renter's insurance," Shiffon smiled, pulling out the brochure she snatched off her mother's kitchen counter.

"Keera, who's that at the door?" Shiffon heard another girl call out and ask.

"Some lady selling insurance," Keera shouted back.

Shiffon continued holding the brochure out, with a fake ass smile on her face, until the mystery voice appeared.

"Insurance?!" she said, grabbing the brochure out of Shiffon's hand and looking at it for a brief second.

"Girl, you know Dino ain't gon' want no damn insurance," Keera laughed.

"You right," the other girl said, laughing too. "Here, we don't need this," she said handing the brochure back to Shiffon.

"Are you sure? Many renters are unaware that property insurance only covers losses to the building itself. Your personal property and certain liabilities however are only covered through renter's insurance," Shiffon explained, like she really did work for Farmers.

"Word, I didn't know that," the girl said, taking the brochure back.

"Tori, give that lady back her brochure. What the hell you need it for?"

"My own damn apartment! Shoot, I got mad nice shit up in there. I ain't know it wasn't covered."

"Please, keep it and thank you for your time."

"You got a business care or something?" Tori asked.

Shiffon pretended to look in her briefcase. "I'm so sorry, I must've left them in my car. But call the number on the back and an agent will be more than happy to assist you. Thanks again and you ladies have a wonderful day!"

"Thanks!"

"My pleasure."

"She was real nice." Shiffon heard Tori say, as she walked away.

"You never told me how your conference went," Dino said to Bailey, while sitting on the edge of the bed, putting on his Nikes.

"It was cool. Typical lawyer stuff."

"You betta be payin' attention. Law school ain't cheap. I want you to be the best defense attorney in ATL."

"How you know I don't wanna be a prosecutor?" Bailey questioned.

"Cause all the money is in gettin' niggas like me off," he joked. "Prosecutors, mind as well work for free."

"So where you off to?" Bailey wanted to know, not giving a damn about a law degree right now.

"You know, work," Dino said, adjusting the drawstring on his gray and black hoodie. He placed his wallet in the side zip pocket, of the matching ribbed bottom cuff relax joggers he was wearing. He set ever outfit off with a baseball cap. Dino would always say his head felt naked without one.

"Work where?" she pressed.

"What's up wit' all the questions? Regular shit. I won't be gone long. We can do dinner tonight." Dino walked over to Bailey, kissing her on the lips.

Dino smells so fuckin' good. He's wearing my favorite cologne too. This nigga always look so fine in his clothes. His body cut, you'd think he be at the gym every muthafuckin' day. Damn I love this nigga so much! Why he gotta be a fuckin' cheat! Bailey screamed to herself.

"You should let me ride around with you...like we used to do. Be yo' partner in crime," she smiled, becoming wistful.

"Not today, bae. I'll see you later on tonight for dinner."

Bailey didn't know if she wanted to jump out of bed and punch her man in the face, or burst out crying begging him to stay. The pain and anger was real but so was the love.

"Oh shit! I ain't even hear my phone ringing," Baily said out loud, when she noticed Shiffon was calling her. "Hey!"

"Can you meet me?"

"Sure...when?"

"Now. I did a drive by today and we have some things to discuss."

"Okay. Text me where to meet you and I'm on the way." Bailey hung up and her heart was racing. She threw on some jeans, a t-shirt, one of Dino's baseball caps and she was out the door.

"Why you wanna meet way out here?" Bailey questioned, when she arrived at the diner in North Decatur.

"It ain't that far," Shiffon said, taking another bite of her pancake. "But I'm being cautious. I want to make sure nobody see us together."

"That's smart," Bailey nodded. "You're looking very businesswoman like," she said noticing the pencil skirt and blouse Shiffon was wearing.

"But what's up with the church lady wig?"

"It's called a disguise, so what's you're excuse? You looking like you just dragged yourself out of bed."

"I kinda did."

"Would you like some of my pancakes? They're super good," Shiffon offered, pouring a little more syrup.

"No. I can't think about food until you tell me what happened today. So spill," Bailey sniped.

"Okay, so this little attire was for the benefit of my drive by today. Thank fuckin' goodness I did do it because there were two people at that apartment."

"What?! Did they catch you in there?"

"No because I knocked first. Again, thank goodness I had a plan. I told them I was selling renter's insurance."

"Wow, very smart. You're kinda good at this," Bailey remarked.

"You don't spend a couple years living with one of the biggest drug dealers in Philly and not learn some shit. But that's beside the point. This ain't gonna be as easy as you said."

"It was probably just some niggas who work for Dino, stopping through to pick up drugs or something. I didn't think nobody knew where the spot was but our plan is still doable," Bailey huffed. "Don't back down now."

"It wasn't no niggas there. It was Tori and some other chick named Kecia or something."

"You mean Keera?"

"Yeah Keera. I guess you know her too."

"I'ma be sick. I'll be right back." Bailey ran off to the bathroom.

"Excuse me!" Shiffon called out to the waitress. "Can you bring a glass of water and some of your fresh squeezed lemonade."

It took about ten minutes but Bailey finally reappeared. She looked even more disheveled than when she first arrived to the diner. Her eyes were bloodshot red but it wasn't from drinking.

"Girl, were you in there crying?" Shiffon asked, pushing the glass of lemonade towards her cousin.

"Thanks for ordering this for me," Bailey said taking a sip.

"I figured you would need it when you ran off to the bathroom."

"I feel so embarrassed." Bailey put her head down. "But when you mentioned Keera, it was all too much."

"Is she supposed to be one of your besties too?"

"I sure know how to pick my friends," Bailey shook her head disgusted. "How didn't I see both Tori and Keera were snakes. Is Tori living at the apartment?"

"No. There wasn't any furniture there but a couch, like you said. Plus, Tori mentioned she had her own place. My guess is, Dino got them doing some work for him," Shiffon reasoned.

"So that hoe fuckin' my man and workin' for him. To think, I was actually considering giving Dino another chance," she admitted.

"Bailey, we don't have to do this. Real talk, I get it. I'm your cousin. You don't have to play the tough girl role wit' me. You still love that nigga." Shiffon stated, with no hesitation.

"I do but I hate that muthafucka too. Like how he do this shit to me. Is he fuckin' that bitch raw! I wanna stab that nigga," Bailey fumed.

"Keep your voice down." Shiffon said, looking around, making sure no one was ear hustling on their conversation.

"How the fuck can I calm down when my two best friends and my man are stabbing me in the back."

"Listen, I don't mind listening to you vent but before you continue, do you or don't you want me to move forward with the plan?" Shiffon wanted to know.

"Hell fuckin' yeah and I want to add something to it."

"What?"

"I'll pay you double, if you kill Tori and Keera too."

Shiffon was about to spit out her water. "Did I hear you say kill?" Shiffon mouthed in a low voice. "You make it sound like you just adding ice cream to your grocery list."

"Don't act like you ain't never killed somebody before," Bailey mumbled under her breath.

"That ain't the fuckin' point!" Shiffon spit back.

"Then what is? I said I would pay you double."

"Are you gonna do that double life sentence for me if I get caught?"

"Cousin, you ain't gonna get caught. If anyone

can pull this off, it's you.." Bailey stated with confidence.

"Do I look like a fuckin' assassin to you!"

"What does that mean?" Bailey was perplexed by Shiffon's statement.

"You want to hire me to kill someone...make that two people. That's what assassins do."

"Oh, I thought the person assassins killed had to be important," Bailey cracked.

"Clearly, them broads important to you, right," Shiffon spit. "Cause if they wasn't, you wouldn't be willing to pay me to kill them."

"You've made your point. So, will you do it or not?" Bailey wasn't backing down from her request. "You know them hoes deserve to die! I treated them like they was my sisters. They've betrayed me in the worse way."

"Killing Tori and Keera won't mend your broken heart, Bailey. This is me talking to you as your cousin."

"I know but trust, it will help me sleep better at night. I got something for Dino's ass too but I want to handle him personally. So are you in or not?" Bailey stared intently, waiting for her cousin's response.

"I'm all in for the robbery but I'ma have to think hard about murder."

"What do..."

Shiffon put her hand up, cutting her cousin off. "Bailey, don't push me on this," she warned. "I said I'll think about it."

"Fine." Bailey was aware her cousin didn't respond well to badgering. As much as she wanted to continue pleading her case, she knew if there was any chance of Shiffon killing her former best friends, she needed to back off.

Chapter Four

ALL IN

"Tori, have you decided what you want to do for your birthday?" Bailey asked, while they shopped at Phipps Plaza.

"Not yet. I'm waiting to see what my friend got planned for me," she replied coyly, eyeing an ice blue glitter beaded mini dress.

"Girl, what's your friend name? You been spending mad time with him," Keera laughed.

Tori and Keera eyed each other and Bailey knew it was them sharing, what they believed to be an inside joke about her man. She wanted to read them for filth but decided to remain committed to her plan.

"Tori, you got a new man? How you keeping secrets from your besties!" Bailey smiled widely. "Unless you already know all about him...do you Keera?"

"Me...nah! I don't know nothing about him." Keera had to catch herself from sounding shocked and nervous at Bailey's question.

"I have a great idea. Why don't you, me, Dino and your new friend go out for a double date?" Bailey suggested.

"The relationship is still kinda new," Tori replied. "We're still getting to know each other."

"How new?" Bailey wanted to know as her insides boiled.

"A few months," Tori said, glancing over at Keera.

"Keera, have you met him, yet...how does he look?" Bailey saw the goofy stare on Keera's face disappear.

"No, not yet. I just said I don't know nothing about him," Keera hissed.

"You ain't gotta get all defensive." Bailey stopped in the middle of the store and popped. "You actin' like you got something to hide."

"You trippin'," Keera giggled. "Tori's mentioned him a few times but she's keeping dude a secret for now."

"I see. Well hopefully you'll share this mystery man with us soon. But in the meantime, I booked the three of us a spa treatment at that new place over on Ashford Dunwoody Road," Bailey informed her frenemies.

"I heard that place is supposed to be super nice!" Tori said cheerfully.

"Yeah, I thought it would be a great pre birthday celebration. Of course, it's my treat. I got us the grand spa experience package."

"Wow, sounds expensive!" Keera exclaimed.

"It is. I guess we should be thanking Dino, since technically he's footing the bill. But only the exclusive shit for my two best friends," Bailey winked.

"I can't wait! I love being pampered," Tori gushed with excitement. "First the spa, then I can get all cute for my boo." Tori gave a mischievous smile, holding up a sheer, lacy teddy with a sexy v-wire plunge neckline. "He'll go crazy seeing me in this!"

"Damn sure will," Keera agreed, admiring the lingerie Tori decided to purchase.

These dirty lowdown hoes. This heffa showing off the lingerie she plans on seducing my man in. Like what the fuck type of scandalous shit is this. How can I have been this dumb? All these years I'm believing we sisters while Tori was plotting on my man and Keera cheering her on. Fuck hiring Shiffon, I might have to kill these bitches myself, Bailey seethed.

"Ma, what you over there looking for?" Shiffon casually asked when she walked into the kitchen. Noticing her mother flipping through some mail on the counter.

"I was just looking for this brochure, I could've sworn I left it over here."

"Brochure?"

"Yeah. It's just a brochure for renters insurance," Shiffon's mother said, continuing to look.

"My fault, I gave that to a chick I know. I thought it was junk mail."

"Don't worry about it," her mother waved her hand as if it was no big deal, opening the refrigerator.

"Why would you need a brochure about renters insurance? You own this house," Shiffon couldn't help but ask, sitting down to eat her cereal.

"I've been thinking about downsizing and moving into an apartment."

"Downsizing? It's only a two bedroom house. How much more downsizing can you do...what is Milo gonna sleep on the couch with me now?"

"No, I would get a two bedroom but I wouldn't have to deal with no yard work or nothing. A lot less maintenance. That sort of downsizing."

Shiffon wasn't buying her mother's explanation. "Ma, what's really going on? You love this house.

I remember when you and Daddy bought it a year before he died." She stated sadly, hating to reflect back to that time in their lives.

Her mother walked slowly over to the kitchen table and took a seat across from Shiffon. "I didn't want to have to tell you this but our house is in foreclosure."

"What! Why are you just now telling me this?"

"After Clay went to prison and you having to move back home, you ain't been the same. There was no sense in adding to your stress."

"But I might've been able to help."

"Help how, Shiffon? You ain't got no money."

Tears swelled up in Shiffon's eyes. Hearing her mother say those words were painful. She'd always been the one person her mother could call and get anything she needed. After Shiffon's father died, she kept a man with some money. She had wanted to provide the financial support for her mother and little brother that was now lacking due to her father's sudden death. This was the first time in her young adult life, Shiffon felt helpless.

"How far behind are you?" Shiffon questioned.

"Too far to catch up now," her mother shook her head. "A few months ago my hours got cut at work. I've been working a second job but without..." her voice trailed off.

"Say it. Without my help you haven't been able to manage paying your mortgage and the rest of the bills. Some daughter I am." Shiffon frowned.

"Chile, stop blaming yourself. This ain't none of your fault. You always did right by me. I shouldn't have become dependent on the money you would give me every month. After your father died, I couldn't afford this house. I should have sold it a long time ago," she reasoned. "Oh well. What you won't do on your own, the man will make you do it." She slapped her hand down on the table and rose up from the table.

"Ma, don't give up just yet. I might be able to turn this around," Shiffon insisted.

"I've known for some time now this day would soon be approaching. I've already shed many tears, so I'm fine. This is new to you and I understand it might be hard for you to accept the inevitable. But we'll get through this, together as a family," she assured her daughter.

"Does Milo know?"

"Not yet. I plan to tell him soon before school starts back."

"Mother please, just give me two weeks," Shiffon pleaded. "If I can't come up with the money, then you do what you have to do."

"Girl, how in the world will you be able to come up with all that money?"

"Clay might have some money for me," Shiffon lied.

"He in federal prison, how he got money for you?"

"This dude who owes him a lot of money is supposed to bring it to me. Clay ain't making no promises but he's pretty sure the dude will come through."

"You still ain't learned your lesson," she sighed. "After all the drama you went through with Clay, I thought you would've realized you can't depend on no man for shit. I'll give you two weeks but it ain't gon' make a damn difference."

Shiffon slumped down in the chair once her mother left the kitchen. Although her mother implored her not to, Shiffon felt an enormous amount of guilt for her family's current situation. Her little brother already had to grow up without a father, for him to have to leave the only home he'd ever known wasn't an option to Shiffon.

"I know exactly how to make this right," Shiffon mumbled while dialing her cousin's number.

"I thought you lost my number. I ain't heard from you since we met at that diner," Bailey remarked.

"I had a lot to think about."

"What did you decide?"

"Do you still want the full course meal...dinner and dessert?" Shiffon proposed to her cousin.

"Absolutely," Baily confirmed without hesitation.

"Then it's on. We can discuss the details later." Shiffon needed a bit of an incentive to come around to seeing things Bailey's way, and saving her mother's house did it.

Chapter Five

SECOND
THOUGHTS

"Yo it took everything for me not to burst out laughing when Bailey was interrogating me about your secret boo," Keera giggled. "That shit was funny!"

"You don't think she knows anything do you?" Tori questioned. "I been feeling a tad uneasy since that day at the mall. Bailey's vibe didn't seem off to you?"

"Hell to the no! The only vibe I got was her typical bougie bullshit vibe. Bailey too far up her own ass to ever notice you and her sharing dick."

"Keera, you ain't right for saying that shit," Tori smirked.

"But am I lying? You and Bailey both riding all them inches. The way y'all brag about that niggas dick, I might have to jump on that muthafucka too," Keera joked, while applying an extra coat of mascara to her mink lashes.

"Nah, bitch, he's off limits. I'm 'bout fed up with sharing Dino with Bailey," Tori confessed as she debated which heel would look best with the white studded, bandage jumpsuit she was wearing.

"I knew you was catching real feelings for that nigga!" Keera turned and blurted to Tori.

"So, what's wrong with that?" Tori shrugged, turning to the side. Eyeing herself in the full length mirror. She decided to go with the open toe rose gold clear stiletto. The extra inch on the heel made her ass sit up just the way she liked.

"Listen, I get why you like Dino...mad chicks do. I also understand why you started fuckin' around wit' him. I even got a good laugh at Bailey's expense, since she swear she better than every damn body. But I thought you was up on enough game to know not to fall in love," Keera huffed.

"Who said anything about being in love?!" Tori became defensive.

"Bitch, I done known you since our hopscotch days. I can read you better than you can read yo'self. Dino got you open."

"I wish I could deny it but maybe he does. It's all good though, cause he open off me too." Tori smiled coyly.

"Oh Lawd!!" Keera jumped out of her chair. "Girl, you know I ain't one to bullshit, so I'ma spit it out. Dino not leaving Bailey for you. Yes her uppity ass irk my nerves but the two of them got a long history. Nah, that nigga ain't neva gonna marry Bailey but he ain't leaving her neither, especially not for her so called best friend." Keera rolled her eyes as if thinking how could Tori be that dumb.

"Talk about cold." Tori sounded like the wind had been knocked out of her and she was deflating.

"You say I'm being cold, I call it a reality check. I would hate for Dino to break your heart but the way you standing over there with that sad ass face, it's inevitable," Keera said, shaking her head.

"Let's discuss this shit later. We 'bout to go out and have some fun. I don't want a Dino conversation putting a damper on our girls night out," Tori grumbled," fluffing out her hair.

"Whatever you say." Keera side eyed her friend as she put the final touches on her makeup. For the past few months she assumed Tori was the one winning. Fuckin' around with a money dude like Dino. Getting all the financial and sexual perks without the emotional headache Bailey constantly dealt with. But Tori made the terrible mistake of catching feelings for an unavailable man. Not only was she the side chick, she was best friends with the main girl, so Tori was reminded of her position on a daily basis. *Talk about being on the losing end...you better get your mind right Tori*, Keera thought to herself.

Damn I love this nigga or maybe I'm just addicted to the dick. Fuck! I think it's both, Bailey reasoned, gripping her legs around Dino's back, wanting to feel all of him against her body. For a man who had been running the streets since he was a kid and rough to the core, Dino had the softest skin of any man Bailey had ever known. He was the prettiest yet hardest nigga you could meet. This combination was proving to be lethal for Bailey.

After catching her man in bed with her best friend, Bailey promised herself she would never fuck Dino again. A promise she broke in less than a week and had since been breaking every damn day. At this point it was a love/hate relationship, except Bailey was the only one privy to all the hate she had towards her man. But for the moment she was in love or better yet lust as Dino's tongue licked her hardened nipples. He had this way of making her feel so beautiful when they made love. He always took his time, making sure each stroke hit her G-spot. The mythical area that brought maximum pleasure and solidified Dino as a masterful lover.

"You tryna put a nigga to sleep," Dino chuckled after Bailey had her second orgasm, but tried pulling him back in bed with her.

"I just don't want you to go. Is there something wrong with that?" Bailey asked.

"Nah, babe." Dino leaned down kissing Bailey on her lips.

"Then get back in the bed with me," she insisted.

"I would but I gotta meet up wit' Nate. We got some business to handle."

"I guess it doesn't make sense for me to wait up for you."

"Nah, I won't be home until late," Dino said heading towards the bathroom to take a shower.

"Maybe I'll hang out with Keera and Tori tonight. We haven't gone out for drinks in a while."

"Okay, babe...but don't have too much fun!" Dino called out as if he had no worries about his woman and mistress poppin' bottles together. This only infuriated Bailey. It was the wakeup call she needed to remain committed to her plan. She grabbed her phone to get confirmation from Shiffon.

Bailey: We still on for Friday?!???!?!

Shiffon: Yep
Bailey: Good!! I'm ready to move the fuck on
Shiffon: Cool...

Shiffon purposely kept her text messages brief. She had already warned her cousin to keep their dialogue limited but Bailey's emotions were constantly getting the best of her. It was to be expected under the circumstances but it was the reason Bailey needed Shiffon to make her move soon before she changed her mind again. There was no denying the hold Dino had on her. Bailey knew getting far away from him was the only way to free herself from his grasp.

"Baby, don't forget about our dinner plans for Friday." Bailey reminded Dino when he got out the shower.

"How I'ma forget. You been reminding me for the last week," he said dropping his towel.

Damn, am I ready to let this nigga go for good, Bailey wondered while watching Dino get dressed. *Look how cut he is. Nothing but muscles. He so fuckin' fine...that body...that face...that dick! Don't fall back in the trap, Bailey...Fuck him and Tori! I love that muthafucka but I have to let him go. The only thing that makes this shit tolerable, is Tori won't be here to relish in taking my place, because that heartless hoe will be dead!* Bailey argued with herself trying to convince her head not to listen to her heart. For the moment, her heart was winning the war.

Chapter Six

TELL THE TRUTH

Shiffon found herself back at her favorite diner in North Decatur. But this time she wasn't meeting her cousin, she was waiting for an old friend named Essence. She recently moved to Charlotte, not by choice but because like Shiffon, her man had gotten locked up by the Feds and the money dried up.

"Dang them pancakes look good. You could've ordered me some," Essence complained the moment she sat down.

"You texted me an hour ago saying you would be here in fifteen minutes. If I had ordered you some food, it would be cold by now," Shiffon smacked.

"I gotta a little lost."

"Nah, you just drive slow. The waitress will be back over in a second and you can order something."

"This food ain't coming out my gas money is it?" Essence wanted to know.

"Girl, nah! The food is on me. You know I ain't petty like that." Shiffon sounded offended.

"Last I heard you was broke just like me. I had to borrow some money from my homegirl because I didn't have enough gas in my car to even make it here. Man, this shit is for the birds. I'm thinking about going back to the strip club," Essence shrugged.

"I feel you. I ain't never worked the pole but it's mos def crossed my mind," Shiffon asserted.

"It's crazy. This time last year we were all living it up at a luxury resort in Bora Bora. Now our niggas is locked up, you sleeping on yo' mama's couch and I'm staying in my homegirl's spare bedroom." Essence shook her head pondering how her world went to shambles so quickly.

"Who you telling but I have a way we can make some coins."

"I know! Do you think I woulda spent money I don't have to get here, if you didn't promise to put some coins in my pocket. All I want to know is how much, cause a bitch is desperate."

"Not sure the exact amount but at least a few stacks," Shiffon confirmed. "It could be more but definitely no less than that," she said, as Essence gave her order to the waitress.

"Works for me."

"You're not gonna ask me what you have to do?" Shiffon questioned after the waitress walked away from the table.

"You already said on the phone I don't have to fuck nobody, so we good. You know I've always been a little particular about who I have sex wit'. If he ain't cute...," Essence reminded her friend.

"I know...I know. Lucky for you, what we have to do has nothing to do with sex, more like murder," Shiffon whispered.

Essence raised an eyebrow, unsure if she heard her friend correctly. "Did you say mu..."

"Yes." Shiffon nodded, not letting her get the word out. "Are you still in?"

"What part of desperate aren't you understand-ing. Listen, I'd be lying if I didn't prefer an easier way to come up on some money but I trust you, Shiffon. As long as we don't get caught. Prison not my thing."

"Mine neither. Trust me, I need this to go smoothly. It's the main reason I want to have backup, which is you."

"Is that the only reason you chose me?" Essence asked.

"Truth be told, there is another reason," Shiffon admitted.

"I know yo' ass too well. Spit it out."

"Your cousin still moves a little weight, right?"

"Yeah, why?"

"If all goes according to plan, we're gonna get our hands on some product. I need a connect who ain't on no bullshit to buy it from us," Shiffon explained.

"How much product you talking about?"

"Again, I'm not sure but from what I understand it supposed to be a decent amount."

"Depending on the amount and how good the product is, I'm sure he'd wanna take it off your hands. But if he can't, the homegirl I'm staying with, her man is a good option. I know he would be good for the money too," Essence assured her.

"Perfect, because that money will be all ours. So your few stacks about to go way up."

A smile spread across Essence's face. The idea of getting her hands on thousands of dollars was the best news she heard in months. Her and Shiffon weren't used to nor did they cope well with the struggle life. Both had tried to enter the workforce, but with no college education and limited skills, their options were nominal. And the offers they did receive barely paid above minimum wage. The women felt stuck, until now.

Bailey turned the volume all the way up when Cardi B's Be Careful came on. She immediately started rapping along, not missing one word.

Look
I wanna get married
Like the Curry's, Steph & Ayesha shit
But we more like Belly, Tommy & Keisha shit
Gave you TLC, you wanna Creep & shit
Poured out my whole heart to a piece of shit

The lyrics to the song resonated with her as Bailey had flashbacks to the first time her and Dino met. She reflected on the many ups and downs they had over the years. It was all pretty much one sided. Dino fuckin' up and Bailey taking him back or better yet staying with him. She never thought she'd leave him until now. While listening to the song, Bailey was falling deeper into her thoughts of heartache and betrayal, until Keera's name popped up on her display.

"This heffa would call right now," Bailey scoffed before answering. "Hey girl! What's up!" she made sure to sound extra chipper. Not wanting to give her enemy the slightest clue she was on her shit list.

"Nothing much. I was hoping you could stop by so we could talk," Keera said.

"Is everything okay? You sound mad serious."

"Can you please just come over, Bailey."

"Sure. I'm on the way." Bailey took the next exit off the expressway. As she got closer to the apartment complex Keera stayed at, she began to feel uneasy. *I know Keera and Tori ain't gonna try and jump me on some tag team shit...or would they? I can't put nothing pass them hussies at this point. Let me bring my stun gun just in case,* Bailey said to herself, reaching inside the glove department.

It only took Keera a hot second to open the door after Bailey knocked.

"Damn that was fast!" Keera exclaimed letting Bailey in.

"Yeah, I was on the expressway headed to the mall when you called. I was coming up on your exit," Bailey explained, eyeing her surroundings to make sure she wasn't about to be bum-rushed.

"That was good timing," Keera said sitting down on the couch.

"Is anybody else here?" Bailey questioned, unable to brush off her uneasiness.

"Nope, it's just us. Can I get you something to drink?" Keera offered.

"I'm good." Bailey sat down on the chair across from Keera and tried to get comfortable but it was a losing battle. She had no trust for her former friend, so Bailey felt the need to keep her guard up. "Your call sounded like some 911 shit. Are you gonna tell me what's going on?"

Keera let out a deep sigh and shifted her body on the couch. "Not sure if you noticed but I've been keeping my distance from you lately."

"Now that you mentioned it, you're right...you have. I guess I've had other things on my mind, I didn't give it much thought."

"Would those things on your mind have anything to do with Dino?" Keera's question took Bailey by surprise.

"Why would you think that?" Bailey's tone was much more belligerent than she intended it to be. She paused and regained her cool. "Dino and I aren't having any problems."

"Listen Bailey, for the last few weeks I've been wanting to tell you something. I knew you'd be furious and you have every right to be."

"Keera, would you stop talking in riddles and tell me what the fuck you have to say!" Bailey popped.

"You have to promise me two things first. You can't let anyone know I told you."

"And what's the second thing?" Bailey asked becoming impatient.

"Don't smack the shit outta me." Keera put her hands up in a playful manner but her face was dead ass serious.

"I promise, now spit it out, Keera!"

"There's no easy way to tell you this. Tori is basically in a full fledge relationship with Dino. They've been fuckin' around now for a few months."

Although Bailey had been privy to this information for a few weeks now, hearing Keera say those words, was even more painful than when she caught Dino in bed with her best friend. It made it all the more real. She couldn't suppress the truth because Keera was shouting it directly to her face.

"When you say months how long?" Bailey wanted to know.

"The night of your birthday when the three of us went out."

"That was like seven months ago. Tori brought me home because I was way too drunk to drive," Bailey recalled.

"Yeah," Keera nodded. "You were passed out upstairs in bed. Supposedly Dino made his move and they had sex downstairs in the living room. They've been messing around ever since."

"I can't believe this." Bailey stood up from the couch. She felt as if she was gasping for air. Keera reacted to her distress by going in the kitchen and grabbing a bottle of water.

"Here drink this," she said, handing the bottle to a distraught Bailey.

"Why are you telling me this...are you trying to hurt me?"

"I thought you had a right to know. I should've

told you when I first found out but..."

"When was that?!" Bailey shouted, cutting Keera off. "How long have you known and don't lie to me."

"A couple months now. I knew Tori was seeing somebody but she was being so hush, hush about it. Then one day I stopped by her place unexpectedly, because I left something over there from the night before. When I pulled up to the parking lot, I saw Dino getting in his car leaving. I confronted Tori and at first she denied and lied until finally admitting the truth. She begged me not to tell you."

"How could you both do this to me! We were supposed to be like this!" Bailey yelled, crossing her fingers tightly.

"I know but I've known Tori since we were kids. Her mom and my mom are best friends. I couldn't betray her."

"But it was okay for you to betray me!" Bailey shot back.

"No it wasn't okay. I felt like shit and still do. Real talk, when I first found out, I thought you were getting exactly what you had coming for actin' like you was better than us," Keera divulged.

"You fuckin' bitch!" Bailey lunged over at Keera and smacked her dab in the mouth.

"You promised not to hit me!" Keera fumed, dabbing a slight bit of blood from the corner of her mouth. "The only reason I'm not gonna smack you the fuck back, is because I deserved that lick for not coming clean from jump. But if you touch me one more time, don't get mad if I strike you back," she warned.

"Y'all was supposed to be my muthafuckin' friends! You wanna excuse that shit cause I acted like I was better than you?!" Bailey seethed.

"I'm not excusing nothing. Tori is dead ass wrong for carrying on wit' Dino. But she's like family to me."

"I thought I was too." Bailey's eyes watered up. She had been so consumed with rage after learning of her two best friend's deceit, she suppressed how despondent she was over their betrayal.

"You are. I love you like a sister," Keera said, walking over to Bailey, trying to hug her.

"Don't touch me." Bailey pushed her away. "You think telling me the truth somehow absolves you of any wrongdoing? It doesn't work like that, Keera."

"Try putting yourself in my position. I love both of you. I swore secrecy to Tori but yet I'm here spilling all her business."

"Are you really spilling it all?" Bailey could see Keera hesitating to answer. "If you ever truly cared about me and you want to salvage what's left of our friendship then tell it all right now," she demanded.

"Of course I want to save our friendship. Why do you think I decided I needed to tell you the truth. I'm praying you'll be able to forgive me."

"If you want my forgiveness then tell me the truth...all of it!" Bailey shouted.

"Besides messing around with him, Tori has also been working for Dino," Keera revealed.

"What sort of work?"

"Tori is a drug courier for Dino. He pays her good money too."

"Is that the reason she's been going out of town a lot these past few months?"

"Partially. A few times she was out of town with Dino. Remember you got tickets for the Drake concert and at the last minute Tori backed out..."

"Yeah, of course I remember. I spent good money on those tickets and I was pissed she couldn't come." Bailey said, recalling the incident.

"Well Dino had to make a trip to Miami and at the last minute he asked Tori to go with him," Keera divulged. "He's also the one who put her up in that townhouse and pays all the bills."

"Oh my fuckin' goodness!" Bailey pressed her hands down on her head as if trying to condense a massive migraine. "That muthafucka! I remember wanting to get us a hotel room near the arena, thinking it would be convenient and Dino flipped out. He told me I better bring my ass home after the concert but he ended up going out of town for the entire weekend. That sneaky nigga was with Tori?!" Bailey wanted confirmation even though she knew the answer.

"Yes but before you ask, I didn't know about their involvement back then," Keera clarified.

"I didn't even put that shit together. And that nigga put her up. He got a full blown mistress," Bailey sobbed. She struggled to make her way to the dining room table. She sat down in the chair and laid her head down on the glass. "Dino ain't shit!" All the rage she had towards Tori and Keera had now shifted to her boyfriend.

"Bailey, you should be furious but please keep my name out of it. I'm afraid what Dino might do if he finds out it was me who told you the truth. I'm not tryna get hurt behind this. Do you hear me?!" Keera raised her voice because Bailey seemed to be in a daze.

"Yes, I hear you and I won't say anything to Dino or Tori," she huffed.

"So what are you gonna do?"

"I'm not sure yet." Bailey glanced down at the diamond ring on her finger. She had fooled herself into believing this was a symbol of their love. She wanted to take off the 7ct brilliant cut stone and flush it down the toilet. Bailey was distraught but hadn't completely lost her mind. When the time was right, she planned on selling the ring for a hefty price. Until then, she had to try to keep her cool.

"Will you ever forgive me?" Keera's tone was contrite. She kneeled down next to Bailey, who was wiping away her tears.

"The lies. I hate all of it." Bailey said between sniffles. "But I'm glad you finally told me the truth. I'm still pissed but yes, I forgive you," Bailey said graciously, as her and Keera hugged each other tightly.

Chapter Seven

LET'S CALL IT OFF

"Girl, I told you I didn't want to see yo' face until after this shit was done," Shiffon hissed, sliding into the booth across from Bailey. "Why are you so pressed to see me?"

"I know but this couldn't wait." Bailey nervously sipped on her ice tea. "There's been a change in plan."

"You have to be fuckin' kidding me! I already have everything in place. I even brought my homegirl down here to help me with this shit. How you gon' flip shit the day before it's supposed to go down!" Shiffon fussed.

"Calm down. The robbery is still a go for tomorrow," Bailey reassured her cousin, glancing around the restaurant. "It's the murder part," she emphasized, lowering her voice.

"Oh, you've had a change of heart about killing your two besties," Shiffon giggled. "I ain't got a problem with that. Them yo' friends, not mine," she shrugged.

"Not so fast." Bailey pushed her glass away. "The murder isn't off. I want Tori gone but not Keera."

"Whatever you say but the pay is the same for one or two." Shiffon made clear.

"The number of people hasn't changed, just the individual."

"If not Keera than who?"

"Dino."

"Girl, stop playing. You said you were taking your share of the money and leaving him for good, although I doubt you'll follow through on that. You've been in love with Dino since forever. No way would you let me kill him." Shiffon cracked, thinking her cousin was joking.

"Do you see me laughing. Dino been playing me for a fool with my supposed to be best friend for months. Do you know he put that bitch up in a townhouse. Not only is he paying all her bills but she's also moving drugs for him. I guess they supposed to be on some Bonnie & Clyde shit. Well those two muthafuckas can die together too," Bailey stated with no remorse.

"Dead is dead, Bailey. I get you hate that nigga right now but if I kill Dino, there's no bringing him back to life." Shiffon spoke very slowly to make sure her cousin understood there would be no turning back once she gave the greenlight.

"I warned that nigga to be careful with me. I want Dino dead."

"Then dead he is." Shiffon nodded her head confirming the women were in agreement.

Tori was on her knees, staring up at Dino with intensity for a few seconds as she deep throated his hardened dick. She then started jacking him off as she sucked the base of his penis, and the top of the balls, right on the urethra. It was almost like a weak suction cup, with a swirl of tongue action. Tori remained steady taking in each inch with every single stroke while staring in Dino's eyes. She'd tighten her lips for a moment and gave the shaft a tiny bite just behind the glans and a little suck. She made sure to add a little gentleness. The longer this went on, the more Dino felt like his dick was being melted in a paradise of warmth, wetness and softness. After letting him fuck her throat as hard as he could, she allowed him to ejaculate in her mouth and swallowed as if Dino's cum tasted like caramel drizzle. Tori's enthusiasm over sucking dick like she needed it, made her mouth seem downright magical.

"Baby, you the best. You suck dick like a champ." Dino patted the top of Tori's head as he got off the bed, like she was his favorite pet.

"You're leaving so soon," Tori said, sitting on the floor naked watching Dino get dressed.

"Yep. I got things to do."

"I was gonna make you something to eat. I'm sure you're hungry."

"I'ma pick some food up while I'm out."

"Dino, please..."

"Stop." Dino put his hand up for a second. "I don't need all that nagging. I get enough of that shit from Bailey."

"I'm sorry. I didn't mean to upset you. Are you coming back over later on tonight?" Tori tried her best not to sound needy but she couldn't' help herself. She'd fallen hard for Dino and keeping him around was her only goal.

"Not sure. I'll hit you up later on and let you know." Dino was a man on the move. He didn't even bother staying around long enough to entertain what Tori planned to say next. He was out the door and headed towards his car when he saw Bailey calling him. "I'll get back to her later," he said, sending her to voicemail.

Dino was preoccupied thinking about the money he was on his way to pick up, he didn't notice the late model silver Altima with dark tinted windows circling the parking lot. If it wasn't for the fact he dropped his car key and had to reach down to pick it up, instead of the three shots ricocheting off the car behind him, half of Dino's face would've been missing.

"What tha fuck!" He roared, diving under his SUV. Dino's heart was thumping as the car accelerated and he could see the skid marks left by the tires. He was about to chance it and take cover in his car but the Altima came back around with guns blazing. Dino wasn't trying to get into a shootout in broad daylight but he knew if he had any chance of making it out alive, he had no choice. He reached in the back of his jeans and pulled out the most powerful yet practical mass market handgun, the Smith & Wesson 500.

Right when the midsize sedan came around the curve, Dino aimed directly towards the front windshield, busting multiple shots causing the glass to shatter. He knew a bullet connected when he heard a loud wail from one of the shooters. The driver sped off and Dino busted off two more shots, to make sure them muthafuckers thought twice about coming back.

"I bet that nigga wit' Tori," Bailey fussed when Dino sent her call to voicemail. She was tempted to drive over to Tori's crib and bust down the door but decided to keep her emotions in check and go home. Then as if her mind was playing a cruel joke on her, Tori called.

"Hello!"

"Hey girl, what you doing?" Tori asked, like she hadn't just got off her knees sucking her best friend man's dick.

"On my way home. How 'bout you?"

"Ready to take a shower. My boo just left. I wanna keep his scent all over my body but a bitch got shit to do, so I gotta clean my ass and get ready to go."

Hoe, is you taunting me on the low?! Bailey wanted to scream through the phone. *Damn she got some balls on her cause she gotta be talking about Dino. That's the only nigga she fuckin' wit. I had a feeling he was with Tori when he didn't answer my call and this heffa just confirmed it,* Bailey fumed.

"Sounds like you got it bad for this mystery guy of yours." Bailey played it cute, only because she knew it was going to get real ugly for Tori very soon.

"Ain't no shame in my game...I do. The nigga

fine, he can fuck and he got money," Tori bragged. "He a keeper."

"Since there ain't no shame, when you gonna let me meet this dude?"

"We still keeping things on the low. He got a girl but they relationship pretty much dead. I'm pretty sure he'll be dumping her soon. Then me and him will be a couple."

"Well be careful with that, Tori. Niggas are notorious for leading chicks on. Making them believe one thing and it's something entirely different. I would hate for your feelings to get hurt. Especially since you got it so bad for the this mystery man."

Thanks for the advice but umm don't forget about our spa treatment tomorrow. I'm excited. I need some pampering!" Tori exclaimed, ready to switch the subject. "I was thinking maybe we could go out for drinks afterwards."

"Girl, unfortunately I can't make the spa treatment. You and Keera will have to go without me. But no worries, everything has been paid for, even the tip. Oh and remember it's an all day thing."

"I've been really looking forward to this spa day, so I appreciate you covering all the expenses even though you won't be there. But why aren't you coming?"

"I totally forgot Dino is taking me out to lunch. He wanted to do something really romantic, we're going to that new restaurant in Buckhead. The one all the ballers be at. Maybe when your mystery boo can be seen with you in public, he can take you there. Or better yet we can double date. What you think?" *Yeah bitch, how it feel, me stabbing yo' trifling ass right back,* Bailey thought to herself.

"Sure, that sounds cool but I gotta go. Talk to you later," Tori said rushing to get off the phone.

"Yeah, I bet yo' dumb ass want to get off the phone," Bailey scoffed as she pulled into the garage. At this point, she didn't know who she hated more, Tori or Dino. Both of them disgusted her. She wasn't home for more than ten minutes when Dino came storming in the house, cursing up a storm.

"I'ma find them muthafuckers and kill 'em!" Dino's voice thundered through the house. He threw a duffel bag he was carrying on the floor.

"What happened...why are you so upset?" It was no secret Dino had a temper on him but she couldn't remember the last time she'd seen him this irate.

"Yo these niggas just tried to kill me!"

"Who...when?!" Bailey's eyes widened. *I just told Shiffon I wanted her to kill Dino. I know she didn't make her move already or did she,* Bailey wondered.

"I bet it's that muthafucka who owe me money. I was on my way to pick up the cash, when somebody pulled up in the parking lot, driving an Altima and started shooting," Dino shouted.

"Did you see their faces?" Bailey questioned, still not hundred percent convinced it wasn't Shiffon.

"Nah but when I tried to call that nigga, he ain't answering. That shit ain't no fuckin' coincidence. I swear on everything, if I find out he had anything to do wit' this shit...that nigga dead,' Dino promised.

"Dino, you need to calm down," she said following him upstairs to their bedroom.

"Fuck calming down. If I ain't have my gun on me, I'd be dead right now."

"I can't believe somebody started shooting at you in broad daylight...where were you?"

"Over there by Rivers Edge," Dino answered taking off his clothes to get in the shower.

"Rivers Edge...doesn't Tori live in that area?" Bailey had been completely engrossed listening to Dino's brush with death saga, she'd forgotten her boyfriend had just come from fuckin' her best friend.

"How the fuck would I know where Tori live," Dino shrugged, going into the master bath with Bailey right behind him.

"I could've sworn you picked me up from there a couple times."

"Nah, I ain't never picked you up from there," Dino countered, stepping into the frameless glass shower. He didn't flinch with his response, and it amazed Bailey how he lied to her with such ease.

"Well, I'm just glad you're okay."

"I won't be okay until I find out who tried to kill me and they dead. Niggas bout to pay up wit' my money and they life."

Not unless you're dead first, Bailey seethed. For the very first time in their toxic relationship, she had no desire to take her clothes off and join Dino in the steamy hot shower. That thin line between love and hate, now tilted over to full fledge fury. She didn't want her man anymore. Bailey finally had enough and emotionally checked out the relationship. The clock was now ticking on Dino's demise.

Chapter Eight

SNAKES SURROUND ME

"Girl, how many times are we gonna go over this plan of yours? I told you I got it. No need to tell me again," Essence whined.

"I don't need no hiccups. We only got one shot at this and it has to be done right," Shiffon asserted.

"Listen, we got this. We going in to get that gwop

and brown sugar, then we out. You better make sure ain't nobody gonna be on the other side of the door when we enter the apartment. Other than that we straight." Essence expressed no worries.

"Trust it's handled but I'm taking all precautions. This is what you'll be wearing." Shiffon tossed a bag filled with clothes, shoes and a wig to Essence.

"What's this?" she asked, taking out the clothes.

"It's a maid uniform. Some of the local cleaning companies have their employees wear them. If we run into anybody, they'll assume we're from one of them, so we don't look suspicious. It'll also allow us to conceal the money and drugs we'll be confiscating," Shiffon added.

"We're bringing cleaning equipment too?" Essence questioned, as she continued examining her attire, wanting to make sure it fit.

"Hell yeah! We can't give off the appearance of authentic maids without the necessary goods to clean up," Shiffon rolled her eyes and said.

"Kudos, bitch!" Essence stood up and high-fived her friend. "You running a legitimate operation here. You good at this. Maybe you should consider making it a full time gig," she winked.

"First, let's see how this shit goes tomorrow."

"You seem nervous," Essence commented while looking in the mirror, playing with the wig.

"I am. I've done a ton of crazy shit but this is different." Shiffon laid back on the bed. "So much is on the line."

Shiffon stared up at the ceiling in the motel room thinking about her mother and little brother. The idea of them having to leave their home, made her stomach hurt. Like it actually cramped up when she thought about it. Her mother was putting on a strong front but she could see the pain in her eyes. When Bailey initially came to her with this scheme, it was a way for Shiffon to get off her mama's couch and have a fresh start. Now it was bigger than that.

Knock...Knock...Knock...

"Oh shit! Who is that?!" Essence jumped, snatching the wig off her head.

Shiffon was completely lost in her thoughts, it took her a second to focus and see who was at the door. "Damn, I forgot my cousin was stopping by," she said looking out the peephole. "Hey, come on in."

"Girl, I know you ain't came up on no real loot yet but I've given you enough money that you can stay in an upscale hotel instead of this dump," Bailey commented. Frowning her nose up at the dingy comforters on the double queen size beds.

"I'ma tell you like I told Essence. Upscale hotels come with upscale security cameras. A flea bag motel like this, even if you call 911 and tell them a murder is going down as you speak, it'll take them at least an hour to show up, if they come at all. Places like this aren't on the radar. Which means, if any hiccups happen in the plan and I become a suspect, it won't be easy to trace our movements," Shiffon rationalized.

"Let me find out you built for this," Bailey grinned. "I guess staying in this dump is worth it, if it means covering yo' ass."

"No doubt. I ain't tryna end up where Clay at." Shiffon plopped down on the bed. "I remember when I first started dealing with Clay, he was so fuckin' meticulous with how he moved. I'd never seen a nigga run his drug business like that. He didn't do nothing without a plan. Once he stopped planning, is when shit went to shambles. Biggest mistake he ever made and it's the reason he locked up now."

"Man, I hope thinking about Clay's predicament ain't making you have second thoughts."

"Bailey, you can stop worrying. The robbery and murders are still on. I'm just trying to learn from Clay's mistakes, so I don't end up in prison," Shiffon explained.

"Glad you mentioned the murders," Bailey said, tossing her purse down, deciding to get comfortable. "Some niggas tried to kill Dino. Supposedly some dude owe him money and figured if he shot him dead then the debt would die with him."

"Tried means Dino must still be alive," Essence cracked.

"Yeah, but when he ends up dead, the streets will probably think it's whoever that dude is that owe him money. Which will get back to the police. They'll be so busy investigating that cat, we won't ever be suspects," Bailey winked.

"True but wit' niggas shooting at him, Dino will have his guard up. It'll be damn near impossible to get close enough to put a bullet in his head," Shiffon predicted.

"Good point. I didn't think about that," Bailey acknowledged. "What do you think we should do? I don't wanna wait on this. After what he's done. Dino has to die."

"And he will. I just have to think of another way to get at him. So stop stressing, Bailey," Shiffon sighed, seeing the flustered look on her cousin's face. "I got this."

"I hope so because if you don't...I might wake up one day, reach under my pillow, grab a knife and stab Dino right in the heart," Bailey stated as if she had it all planned out.

"That won't be necessary, but you better hurry home." Shiffon stood up grabbing Bailey's purse and handing it to her. "You need to get some rest tonight and so do we. Tomorrow is a very busy day and we all need to be on point."

"I'll be ready." Bailey turned back and said before leaving.

"Do you believe her?" Essence questioned after Bailey left.

"Oh, no doubt. She'll do her part and keep Dino busy while we're robbing his apartment."

"I'm not talking about the robbery, I meant the murder. When you first introduced me to your cousin years ago she was wit' that nigga. Now she want him dead. I'm not convinced."

"What I didn't tell you was Dino has been cheating with her best friend. She actually caught them in bed together at her and Dino's crib. Of course they don't know all this."

"What?! You have to be fuckin' kiddin' me! I would want that nigga dead too. How is she even able to be around that muthafucka holding all this shit in!" Essence shook her head.

"Trust me, she's barely holding it together. At first, Bailey was definitely having second thoughts, but after she found out how long they've been involved. And the intimate details about their relationship, she's been fully committed to seeing Dino dead," Shiffon stated.

"Hell, I can't blame her. She needs to get rid of that trifling best friend too," Essence added.

"The best friend won't be coming outta this unscathed. Tori's first on the hit list and then Dino is up next. Now let's go to bed. My Grandma used to always say, you gotta be well rested when you about to get into some shit," Shiffon laughed, turning off the light.

When Keera arrived at Peachtree St. to meet Tori at the Hookah lounge, she assumed shit had finally hit the fan. She was looking forward to hearing all the salacious details on how Bailey cursed her out. All while smoking premium tobacco, munching on some exotic flavorful Persian/Mediterranean cuisine, and sipping potent fresh cocktails.

"Hey girlie!" Tori stood up and kissed Keera on the cheek when she reached the table. "You look so cute," she gushed complimenting her red, double-lined mini dress.

"Thanks! I picked it up the other day at that new boutique on Piedmont," Keera said, sitting down inside the cream colored leather booth.

"I need to stop by there. I keep hearing they have some really nice clothes and shoes," Tori nodded taking a sip of her drink. "So what's been going on with you? We haven't talked in a few days."

"Yeah, I've been helping my mother out at her daycare. She's short staffed because two of the girls who work there have been out sick. So tell me what's been going on with you." Keera leaned forward. "Any juicy drama...have you spoken to Bailey?" Tori was taking too long so Keera decided to push her along.

"I talked to her earlier today. I wanted to remind her about our spa experience tomorrow but she cancelled."

Cancelled! Here it comes. Bailey told her to kick rocks. And she was gonna demolish that ass on sight for fuckin' her man, Keera smiled to herself, as she waited for Tori to confirm what she was thinking.

"Yep. So it'll be just the two of us but luckily Bailey paid for everything, of course using Dino's money," Tori frowned.

"That's it...Bailey didn't say anything else?"

"Oh, you mean why her ass cancelled. Her and Dino are having some romantic date tomorrow. Of course she sounded like she was bragging and trying to rub it in my face. I was tempted to tell her, I just had her man's dick down my throat. That would've shut her up," Tori seethed.

What tha fuck is Bailey waiting on. I been told her about Tori and Dino, yet she ain't said shit. I know I told her not to say nothing but I didn't think she would listen. Instead she paying for us to go to this spa day. I'm fuckin' confused, Keera thought to herself, deciding she needed to order a stiff drink.

"Maybe it's time you let Bailey know." Keera casually suggested, taking a few puffs from the hookah.

"You know what, I would if I wasn't positive Dino would kill me."

"I thought you said he was tired of her?"

"Yeah, he is but Dino has it in his head, Bailey's going to finish law school. Then he'll have his own personal defense attorney in his pocket. It's all so stupid because Bailey hates law school." Tori rolled her eyes.

"You straight with being the side chick while Bailey continues to live in the big house, and brags about all the perks of being Dino's girl?"

"Fuck Bailey and I ain't no side chick!" Tori rebutted.

The wheels were turning in Tori's head. Out loud she was denying being a side chick but that's exactly what she was and she hated it. In her mind, Tori felt prettier, sexier and even smarter than Bailey. She felt she deserved to have a man like Dino, not her best friend. Now all Tori had to do was figure out how to make it happen.

Chapter Nine

CRASH AND BURN

"You sure ain't nobody inside the apartment?" Essence asked as the women were taking the cleaning supplies out the van.

"Bailey confirmed she's with Dino. Tori and Keera are at the spa. We've been monitoring who comes and goes out that apartment for the past week. The only people we've seen was the chick Tori and Dino. Nobody should be there. But that's why we're wearing disguises, to cover our asses just in case," Shiffon reiterated, locking the car door.

The women parked as close as possible to the apartment entrance, making sure to keep their heads down the entire time. Upon reaching the door, Shiffon knocked lightly.

"Girl, you better put yo' back into that knock and make sure if somebody in there, they can hear you," Essence huffed, pounding her fist against the door.

"Are you satisfied!" Shiffon snapped, putting the key into the lock. Once inside, she locked the door and made sure to put the chain on too. If anyone did pop up, Shiffon wanted to make they had time to make their move first.

"This place damn near empty," Essence commented, while holding on to the vacuum cleaner.

"I told you, ain't nothing but that sofa in here. It's used for stashing shit. Let's go see what we're working with." Shiffon said, heading to the bedroom in the back, where Bailey said the cash and drugs were located.

"I don't see nothing," Essence remarked, glancing around the room.

"Because it's in here." Shiffon opened the closet door. She moved two big bags out the way.

"I still don't see shit!" Essence smacked. "I can't

believe we went through all this and ain't shit here!" she yelled.

"Keep yo' voice down." Shiffon demanded.

"You need to call Bailey and find out what the fuck is going on."

"I can't. I didn't bring my cell with me. Phones always be the first thing that mess you up. Maybe there's some sort of hidden compartment under this carpet." Shiffon searched but there was nothing. "Fuck!" She put her hands over her head. She thought about the plans she had for her cut of the money, like stopping her mother from losing the house.

"Girl, this shit is a bust." Essence stated what both of them was thinking. "Let's get outta here before somebody show up. That's the last thing we need," she said walking out the door. Shiffon followed behind, ready to cry because she was so pissed.

As Shiffon was walking down the hall, she noticed a door was shut. She opened it and decided to check that closet too, although Bailey specifically said the very back bedroom. Not surprised but still disappointed it was empty too.

"Hurry up!" Shiffon heard Essence call out.

"I'm coming!" Shiffon was about to walk out the room but stopped herself. Bailey's words began playing in her head. *There's nothing but a sofa in there.* Shiffon turned her head around. "Then where did this bed come from. And this muthafucker look brand new too," she said walking closer.

Shiffon pulled off the comforter and pushed off the top mattress.

"Girl, what the hell are you doing in here...we need to go!" Essence shouted, storming into the bedroom. But her mouth quickly dropped. "OMG!!"

"I found the hidden treasure," Shiffon beamed, staring at all the cash and drugs stashed under the mattress.

"We rich! We rich!" The women screamed in unison jumping up and down in their maids uniform.

"Baby, we had this gourmet meal, yummy dessert at this fancy restaurant but your mind isn't here. It's somewhere else," Bailey lamented, dangling the champagne glass in her hand.

"I gotta lot of shit on my mind. Muthafuckas shootin' at me and the nigga who owe me money still missing. I gotta get this handled." Dino took a final swig of his Hennessy. "Come on let's go," he groaned, slamming down his glass.

Bailey glanced down at her watch as they were heading out. It had been at least three hours since she last spoke to Shiffon. She was leaving the motel on her way to Dino's apartment. Her cousin made it clear she wouldn't make contact again until she finished the job and back at the motel. Since Shiffon hadn't called or text, Bailey began to worry if something went wrong.

"Why don't we go see a movie," Bailey suggested once they were in the car. She wanted to keep Dino busy a little while longer in case for some reason Shiffon needed more time.

"Nah, I ain't in no mood for a movie. I need to release some stress." Dino placed his hand on Bailey's upper thigh and squeezed it. "What I need is right between them legs."

Bailey wanted to vomit. She'd been avoiding having sex with Dino ever since Keera broke down the details of his relationship with Tori. She literally hated the very idea of ever having sex with Dino again.

"Baby, I would love to help relieve your stress but I started this morning," Bailey lied.

"Then maybe you can suck me off when we get to the crib."

"Sure." Bailey smiled sweetly while scheming on how to get out of sucking Dino's dick.

By the time they got home Bailey was feeling antsy. She hadn't come up with a legit excuse as to why she wouldn't be giving him no head. She was scared anyway, her rage might get the best of her, and she'd try to rip his dick off with her teeth.

"Let me go take a shower before I pleasure you baby." Bailey blew Dino a kiss. She was using every opportunity to stall.

"A'ight but hurry up! I'm 'bout to explode," Dino scoffed, pouring himself a drink.

Bailey took her time undressing, dreading what was coming next. *You done sucked this niggas dick a thousand times. Do it and get it over with*, she shouted to herself stepping into the shower. After allowing the hot water to drench her body, she resigned herself to just do it. Bailey got out ready to do the deed. She was lathering her damp skin with lotion, when she became startled by a loud ruckus coming from the bedroom.

"What the hell is going on in here?" Bailey questioned Dino who was opening and slamming shut dresser drawers.

"Where the fuck is my other gun?!" Dino barked, ready to tear the room apart.

"You moved the gun. You put it in the middle drawer in your closet," Bailey reminded him. Dino brushed past her without saying a word. "You welcome," she said sarcastically, when he found the gun right where she told him it would be.

"I'll be back." Dino was breathing heavy like a bull.

"Are you gonna tell me what's going on?" she chased after him down the stairs.

"That apartment where I keep money and drugs."

"What about it?"

"Somebody broke in and stole it all."

"What...do you know who did it?" Bailey pretended to be shocked.

"Nope but I will."

"How?"

"I have a camera set up in there. So I'm 'bout to see exactly who robbed me. Once I know who it is, they gon' regret ever stepping foot in that apartment." Dino rushed out, slamming the front door.

"Oh shit!" Bailey's heart was racing. She ran back upstairs, scrambling to retrieve her phone. She kept calling Shiffon but there was no answer. Bailey was about to send her a text but thought about her cousin's warnings. Instead she threw on some clothes, grabbed her purse and headed out the door to track Shiffon down. Bailey had to warn her they were caught on tape. Even if Dino didn't recognize them, she was almost positive Essence and Shiffon said something that would easily identify who they were.

Chapter 10

GUILTY
CONSCIOUS

"Tell me exactly what happened and don't skip over shit!" Dino growled at a visibly shaken Tori. She hadn't stopped pacing the living room floor since entering the apartment, and finding it in disarray.

"Dino, I already told you," she said nervously.

"Tell me again!" Dino's loud voice echoed in Tori's ears.

"Keera and I left the spa. It's not too far from here. We were on our way to get something to eat but Keera's mom called and she had to go. We were supposed to meet back up a little later to have some drinks and dinner. Since I was already in the area, and where we were meeting later on was near here too, I decided to come, change my clothes and chill for a little bit." Tori explained for the fifth time.

"When you got here was the door open or unlocked?"

"No it was locked. I didn't realize anything was wrong until I noticed the bedroom door was cracked open. I remember it being completely shut last time I stopped by. At first, I thought maybe you had come by but when I pushed the door open, the mattress and comforter were on the floor. That's when I called you."

"You bet not be bullshittin' me, Tori." This time Dino wasn't yelling. His voice eerily calm but he placed his large hand around Tori's delicate neck.

"Dino, I swear! I had nothing to do with this. I would never steal from you. Never!" She cried.

Dino began to press down on Tori's neck, squeezing it tightly. Her eyes widened in fear and she tried screaming out but nothing would come out. She was kicking her legs as Dino lifted her petite frame off the floor. Tori knew she was about to die.

Bailey pounded on the motel room door wildly. Her adrenaline was running rampant and she was ready to kick the door in.

Shiffon flung open the door. "Girl, what in the fuck is wrong wit' you?!" she peeped her head out, glancing from side to side making sure Bailey's erratic behavior hadn't drawn unwanted attention. "Get in here!" she pulled her cousin inside the room.

"I've been blowing up your phone. Why haven't you called me back?" Bailey sounded frantic.

"Would you please calm the fuck down! You making my nerves itch," Shiffon huffed. "I was gonna call you when I got to my mother's house. I didn't want any phone communication between us for at least a few more hours."

"Where's Essence?"

"In the shower. She's about to leave. She has to make a quick trip back to North Carolina. Now can you please tell me why you actin' like a mad woman?"

"You have to get outta town! If Dino doesn't already know you're the one who robbed him, then he will soon. And he's gonna kill you," Bailey warned. Her eyes were filled with tears. She looked petrified which scared the shit out of Shiffon.

"How did he find out?" Shiffon swallowed hard.

"He had a hidden camera set up in the apartment.

Shiffon, I swear I didn't know. I would've never put you in danger like that," Bailey cried.

Shiffon slumped down on the bed and closed her eyes. She remained quiet not uttering a word.

"Hey, Bailey," Essence waved, coming out the bathroom with a towel wrapped around her body. "What the hell is wrong with Shiffon? I know she ain't fell asleep like that," she giggled.

"Girl, I was saying a prayer, cause Bailey came in here and damn near gave me a heart attack," Shiffon told Essence.

"I'm still about to have a heart attack! Both of you need to get out of town asap!" Bailey insisted.

"I'm about to hit the road but what's the rush?" Essence asked.

"Dino has a hidden camera in that apartment. He got everything on film including y'all robbing him." Bailey was on the verge of sobbing again.

"Oh that." Essence shrugged, walking over to get her suitcase. "You mean he had a camera."

"Thank Essence for peeping it," Shiffon nodded.

"Man, Shiffon had me waiting forever. I wanted to see what time it was. So, I was standing in the living room and I glanced over at the clock on the wall. Few minutes I look again, and it's still stuck on the exact same time. But then I went back to see what was going on with her and I saw all that cash and money."

"But luckily, even with all our excitement, Essence hadn't forgotten about that fuckin' clock." Shiffon clapped her hands together, showing a sigh of relief on her face.

"I ain't gonna lie...I almost did forget. We were taking out the last bag and something made me look over at the clock one last time. It was still stuck at the same time and I was like hell nah!"

"My ass was tryna drag her out. We had hit the jackpot, so I was ready to go. But Essence would not budge," Shiffon cracked.

"I couldn't shake this feeling. At first I thought maybe it was broke but it looked brand new. I walked closer to the clock, that shit wasn't ticking or nothing. I put my face all up in that mug and there it was. I saw the camera."

"I snatched that camera off the wall so damn quick!" Shiffon laughed. "Then we searched all through that apartment and took anything we even thought might be a surveillance device."

"You ain't lyin'. That shit had us paranoid," Essence chimed in, laughing too.

"Thank goodness!" Bailey beamed. Running over to hug her cousin tightly and then Essence. "I would've never forgiven myself if anything bad happened to the two of you."

"We're glad you care so much but you can relax," Shiffon reassured her cousin, hugging her again.

"I don't ever want to be scared like that again,"

Bailey shook her head, sitting down in the chair. "My heart still racing."

"I understand but hopefully this will make you feel better." Shiffon reached under the bed. "This is your cut." She handed Bailey a bag full of money. "We found a ton of drugs but remember you said that was all mine."

"I remember and you deserve it, Shiffon. I could've never pulled off what you did. I wouldn't have enough nerves," Bailey conceded.

"Don't forget about me!" Essence spoke up and said, before heading back in the bathroom to get dressed.

"My bad, Essence. You played a major role too," Bailey smiled.

"Yes she did. Essence also found a buyer for the drugs. That's one of the reasons she's going to North Carolina," Shiffon told her.

"Now that you've come into this money, I hope you're not gonna forget everything else."

"Bailey, you hired me to do a job and I'm gonna do it. I got you covered. Tori first and then Dino." Shiffon guaranteed her.

"Have you decided how you're gonna take care of Dino?" Bailey wanted to know.

"Yes. Again, I have to give props to Essence. She's turning out to be an even better partner in crime than I expected. Another reason she's going to North Carolina is because there's this white chick she knows named Cora. Her brother has a meth lab, so she's into chemicals and shit."

"Okay...so what y'all gonna do, poison Dino?" Bailey stared at Shiffon dumbfounded.

Shiffon burst out laughing. "Nah, we ain't gonna poison the nigga. Cora is gonna make a car bomb."

Bailey's eyes got super big. "Wow! A car bomb. You really are on some 007 Assassin type shit!"

"I know right." Shiffon smirked. "Dare I say it but I'm enjoying this gig of mine. It's like the ultimate high." You could detect a tiny bit of shame in Shiffon's voice but mostly excitement. She wasn't ready to admit it out loud but Shiffon was secretly imagining her life as a full time assassin.

Chapter Eleven

KILLER
INSTINCTS

"Girl, I can't believe Dino almost killed me," Tori cried, puffing on her third Newport. The thing was, Tori enjoyed Hookah but she wasn't even a cigarette smoker. But for some reason, whenever she was about to have a nervous breakdown she would smoke an entire pack.

"Tori, you need to chill. You've been rambling nonstop ever since you got here, and I still don't know what happened," Keera said, opening a window to help bring a breeze into the room. "Now slow down and tell me exactly why Dino wanted to kill you," she continued while grabbing an odor eliminating spray to try masking the stench.

"I'm sorry if the smell is bothering you but it's the only thing that will calm my nerves," Tori sighed, lighting up another. The incessant shaking of her hand made Keera worry she was going to drop her cigarette and burn a hole in the carpet.

"It's fine just stop pacing the floor and sit down." Keera guided Tori to a chair, and placed a glass ashtray on her lap.

"Thanks. Instead of me going on another long-winded tangent, let me sum it up for you. Somebody broke into Dino's apartment and stole all the money and drugs. And..."

"He thought you had something to do with it," Keera said finishing Tori's sentence. "That is fucked up," she agreed.

"He was literally choking the life outta me. I thought I was gonna die." Tori was still traumatized from her brush with death.

"What made him finally stop?"

"I think my denial even after his nonstop torture, made him finally believe I was telling the truth. But it should've never come to that. I thought Dino trusted me. And loved me too." Tori confessed in a meek tone.

"Dino should've never treated you like that." Keera sat next to Tori and hugged her. "Stress got the better of him and he took it out on you. And no I ain't excusing what he did because Dino knows how loyal you are to him."

"It's like don't none of that shit even matter. I have to make Dino understand I will always have his back. I would never cross him. I love him too much."

The tears began streaming down Tori's face and all Keera could do was give her friend a shoulder to cry on. She had it bad for Dino and there was nothing anyone could do about it.

"Let me try calling him again." Tori put out her cigarette and grabbed her cell phone. "He's still sending me to voicemail," she whimpered. "It's been days. I thought he would've forgiven me by now."

"Forgiven you for what?! You didn't do anything wrong, Tori!" Keera scolded, becoming frustrated. "I know all that crying done made you hungry. Why don't we go get something to eat before it gets too late," she suggested.

"You're right. I'm actually starving. I need a drink too."

"Me and you both. Let me grab my purse and we can head out. And stop calling Dino!" Keera called out, on her way to her bedroom.

Of course Tori didn't listen to her friend's advice. She continued calling and texting Dino, begging him to reply. Tori knew she needed to put her phone away but she couldn't stop herself. She had not self control.

"Come on!" Keera grabbed Tori's arm. "Hopefully some food and drinks will erase Dino out of your mind. Even if only temporarily," she said locking the front door. "It feels so good out here," she commented as they walked towards her car. "It's warm with the perfect breeze."

"I guess," Tori shrugged, sluggishly following behind Keera. Her mind was only consumed on one person. "Oh wait! My phone's ringing. I bet it's Dino!" She instantly perked up, answering without even looking at the caller's name. "Hello!"

"Hi, Tori."

"Oh hey." All the perkiness evaporated from her voice.

"You sound disappointed it's me. Were you expecting someone else...maybe Dino?" Bailey's delivery was so sugary sweet, Tori wasn't sure how to respond.

"Bailey, you're so silly," she stuttered and said.

"I've known for a long time you been fuckin' my man. Hope the dick was worth your life. Bye...bye you weak bitch!"

Before Tori even had an opportunity to address her former best friend's accusations, the call ended and a dark figure, with a hoodie pulled low was standing in front of her. Tori was staring down the barrel of a gun. Two bullets to the chest laid her to rest. The shooter turned, aiming the gun in Keera's direction who was screaming hysterically. She knew she was next but instead the person ran off, disappearing into the darkness.

Shiffon's breathing was rapid. She had done her share of dirt before but running up on someone, staring them in the eyes before killing them in cold blood was a first. Once far away from the scene of the crime she'd just committed, Shiffon reflected on the possible repercussions. Getting caught was surprisingly not one of her concerns. She'd been keeping a watchful eye on her prey once the robbery was a success. Shiffon had been patiently lying in wait for the perfect opportunity to take Tori out. When she saw her arrive at Keera's place, which was located in a mix of apartments and condos nestled on a quiet street, Shiffon knew it was time to make her move.

Per her request, Shiffon placed a call to her cousin before it all went down, using a throw away phone. It was important to Bailey that the person she once thought of as a sister, not only heard her voice, but was aware she knew the truth about her relationship with Dino, before she died. Everything went smoothly and as planned. Shiffon could've easily killed Keera too but Bailey had spared her life. Since she was hired to do a job, Shiffon respected her cousin's wishes.

"Hey baby! I was starting to think you wasn't coming home tonight," Shiffon's mother smiled when she walked through the door.

"I had a few drinks with a friend."

"Dressed like that?" she remarked, eyeing her daughter's gray hoodie and black sweatpants.

"It was a real casual sports bar. Very last minute. I went after leaving the gym. I thought you would be in bed by now." Shiffon sat down on the couch across from her mother.

"Chile, I couldn't sleep."

"Are you not feeling well...is something wrong?" Shiffon was immediately concerned.

"More like everything is right. Baby girl, I still can't believe you came through with all that money to save our home. I can't sleep cause I'm so happy," she laughed.

"Oh Ma. I'm glad you happy but don't scare me like that. We already loss Daddy, we can't lose you too."

"Girl, you worry too much. I ain't going nowhere." She patted Shiffon on her leg. "I didn't wanna tell you this but I put a deposit on an apartment."

"Why?"

"Because I didn't believe Clay was gonna come

through with the money you were expecting. He let you down so many times, I wasn't about to allow him to let me down too. Now I feel guilty," she chuckled. "But hell, that boy owe you. I'm glad he finally did right by you."

Shiffon hadn't seen her mother smile this hard in forever. But she couldn't help but be flooded with shame knowing she'd lied about where the money came from. Giving Clay credit was still a better option than admitting the truth.

"How about we not talk about Clay or the money and be thankful you and Milo don't have to leave the home daddy wanted you to have so bad."

"That's a great idea baby girl," Shiffon's mother winked. "You up to watching a movie together like we used to do when you were little, and followed me around everywhere?"

"I would love to."

Watching television with her mother and seeing how happy she was, made any reservations Shiffon had about her actions, dissipate. As long as she could justify her actions, she had no qualms about being an assassin. Murdering Tori, had unleashed Shiffon's killer instincts.

Chapter Twelve

BAD BITCHES ONLY

"I'm so sorry for what happened to Tori, Ms. Dawson," Bailey said, hugging Tori's mother at the funeral reception she was having at her home.

"Thank you, love. I know how close the two of you were. You girl's shared everything." Ms. Dawson smiled warmly.

You have no idea. All that sharing is what got your whorish daughter killed, Bailey thought continuing to lovingly embrace Tori's mother.

"Yes we did, and it breaks my heart she's no longer here with us," Bailey lied. "If you ever need anything, don't hesitate to call me."

"Thank you, love. I've always thought of you as a daughter. Make sure you still stop by and visit Mama Dawson sometimes."

"I will," Bailey promised, kissing her on the cheek, before going over to sit with Keera.

"Poor Ms. Dawson," Keera shook her head. "Her oldest son got killed a year ago and now Tori. I don't know how much more that woman can take."

"I know what you mean. That's why I told her if she needed anything to let me know. We have to look out for family," Bailey said, taking a bite from her plate of food. "Ms. Dawson sho' can cook. This food is delicious."

"Ms. Dawson can cook," Keera agreed. "I'm surprised you still look at her as family though knowing what Tori did," she uttered.

"Tori was fucking my man, not her Mama." Bailey glanced over at Keera and stated. She then eyeballed Dino, who was in a deep conversation with one of Tori's uncles.

"Did you ever have a chance to confront Tori about her relationship with Dino? I could've sworn I heard her say your name right before she got killed."

"I'm sure you did. From what I've been told, I called her right around the time of the shooting. Can you believe I might've been the last person Tori spoke to before she died. That's crazy," Bailey said as if amazed, slowly shaking her head.

"Yeah that is crazy. So what did you all talk about?"

"I invited her to have brunch with me the next day. I was finally ready to have a face-to-face, and ask her why she would betray me. It's unfortunate I never had the chance. But I forgive Tori. Now if I can only learn to forgive Dino." *It'll never happen. That nigga got next,* Bailey smiled, relishing in the thought.

"Shiffon, thank you so much for splitting the money we got from the drug sale with me.

"You earned it. You found us a legitimate buyer. It's a small world though. I can't believe he's done business with Dino in the past."

"True but I'd forgotten my homegirl met her boyfriend here in ATL. One weekend, she worked a special event at this strip club, so it makes sense."

"You're positive he didn't know the drugs you sold him were stolen from Dino?" Shiffon verified again.

"Yes. Dino has bought drugs from him in the past

but he hasn't heard from him in a while. We're good. Stop worrying. Now back to you." Essence pointed her finger at Shiffon. "You didn't have to do what you did for me. We agreed from jump I would only get twenty percent," she continued, as the women ate pancakes at Shiffon's favorite diner. "And I was more than cool with that."

"I know but you've really been my ride or die on this. I wanted you to know how much I appreciate it. With my share, it's still enough to rent me a cute apartment and put a down payment on a car."

"With the cash you and Bailey split, you should have enough to buy you a nice car."

"There was a very expensive bill I needed to pay off, and I used my portion of the cash to do so."

"Damn, what bill was that? It ain't like you got student loans or nothing."

"It was actually for my mother," Shiffon told Essence. "Best money ever spent," she smiled. "But I'm good. For the last few months I've been sleeping on the couch. Now I'm about to have my own crib. Baby steps but at least it's something."

"I feel you. Girl, for the first time since Bezo got locked up, I don't feel like a broke bitch. I'm tryna hold on tight to my lil' coins. Who knows if we'll ever get another come up like this."

"It's funny you mention that. I've been thinking of a way we can keep the money flowing. And before you call me crazy, hear me out."

"I'm listening." Essence bit down on a piece of bacon dipped in maple syrup.

"What if we started our own business."

"What kind of business?"

"Professional assassins."

Essence burst out laughing but Shiffon wasn't laughing with her. "Wait...you serious?" Essence swallowed hard. "Our business would be killing people. How does something like that even work?"

"Clearly there's a market for our services. We would just have to find a discreet way to get the word out."

"Man, I don't know, Shiffon." Essence frowned.

"Tell me you haven't had a little fun doing this job."

"Actually I've had a lot of fun, and enjoyed the money we made even more but there's no telling what type of gigs we'd get, if any at all."

"Listen, we can pick what jobs we want. I'd be lying if I said some won't be better than others but I think if we do this right, we'll be in high demand. Can you imagine a group of bad bitches that's assassins!" Shiffon boasted.

"What group...it's only two of us."

"For now but I see us expanding. Adding some more bad bitches to the clique. You don't see my vision?" Shiffon questioned.

"Honestly I do," Essence nodded. "Real talk, I think the shit would be dope. Some sexy ass chicks killin' muthafuckas," she giggled.

"OMG, and I got the perfect name for our crew. Bad Bitches Only. Cause we only letting bad bitches in our clique," Shiffon winked.

"I like." Essence grinned widely. "You might be on to something, Shiffon."

"I know I am. The biggest hurdle is letting the right people know about our services but I do have an idea.

"What's that?" Essence listened carefully.

"There's a dude I know, who provides all types of services for people when they come in town."

"What kind of services?"

"If niggas wanna buy some pussy, he can get them any type of chick they request. Hard to get tickets for sports events, concerts, all sorts of shit. He's like a one stop shop for a multitude of things. Why not add us to the list. To make it worth his while, we can give him a small finder's fee for any clients he's able to secure on our behalf," Shiffon explained.

"You've really thought this out, haven't you."

"You can tell right. All I need to know is if you'll be my first bad bitch." Shiffon gave her friend a devilish grin.

"Girl, you know I'm all in!" Essence raised her hand as they hi-fived each other."

"Then Bad Bitches Only is in business!"

It had been over two weeks since Tori's funeral and now Bailey was counting down the hours until Dino would meet the same demise. She was resting peacefully in bed. Her heavy eyelids were halfway close, when she felt a cold hand glide down her inner thigh. Bailey had to fight the urge to shove Dino's arm away. Instead she tried to pretend she was in a deep sleep. It didn't stop Dino from sliding his finger inside the warmth of Bailey's pussy.

Bailey twisted her body to force Dino's finger to stop violating her. She mumbled and twisted her lower body a bit more, so he'd infer she was in a stupor and had no idea what was going on. But Dino had other ideas.

"Wake up!" Dino belted, shaking Bailey.

"What's wrong...is everything okay?" she mumbled with her eyes still closed, staying committed to the notion Dino was interrupting her sleep.

"It's about to be okay," Dino stated, prying Bailey's legs open.

"Baby, not now. I'm sleep."

"Fuck that! I want some pussy," he demanded like he was ordering a piece of meat.

"In the morning." Bailey turned to the side, keeping her eyes shut but he wasn't backing down.

"What tha fuck is going on wit' you? You been

off for the last few weeks. Dodging this dick every chance you get. Is you fuckin' another nigga?!" Dino clenched Bailey's arms tightly. There was no pretending to sleep through that shit.

"NO!! Where is all this coming from?"

"Don't play stupid wit' me, Bailey. You used to wanna ride this dick every chance you could get. Now you act like you scared. Either you fuckin' another nigga, or something else is poppin' off. Now which is it?" his accusatory stare was borderline sinister.

"Baby, I've had a lot on my mind. I've been worried about you getting shot at and robbed. Then Tori being murdered. Sex hasn't been on mind."

"I'll put it on yo' mind again." No more words were spoken. Dino thrusted his hardened dick inside of Bailey and she took it without putting up a fight. Knowing this would be the last time Dino would ever be inside her again, was the only reason Bailey found this nightmare tolerable.

Chapter Thirteen

BYE...BYE DINO

Bailey forced herself to stay in bed until she was positive Dino left the house. To ease her mind, she jumped out of bed and double checked he was gone. She then reached for her cell, desperate to get her cousin on the phone.

"Hello."

"Thank goodness you answered! Please tell me by tonight Dino will be dead. Dino must die! I can't go another day sleeping in the same bed with that man," Bailey yelled.

"What has he done now? Did you find out he's fuckin' another one of your friends?" Shiffon teased.

"No! Worse...he raped me!" She wailed.

"Bailey, I'm so sorry. I had no idea things had gotten that ugly. I would've never made such an insensitive joke."

"It's not your fault. I've allowed myself to be a complete dummy for him. He's played me for a fool all these years. But this time, I'll get the last laugh. The joke will be on Dino."

"Try to keep yourself busy for the rest of the day. I'll be in touch once everything is done. But relax, Bailey. Dino is no longer you're problem. I got you covered," Shiffon assured her cousin before hanging up.

Shiffon wasn't bullshitting Bailey either. She'd been preparing for this day even before killing Tori. She not only kept a watchful eye on Dino, she studied his movements meticulously. Shiffon knew she couldn't afford to make any mistakes. This had to be done right the first time and thanks to Essence hooking her up with Cora, she was confident all would go smoothly.

"Fuck! Please don't let this be Bailey calling back to tell me something else has happened," Shiffon fussed out loud, reaching for her phone. "Hello."

"It's done and ready." That's all that was said

and the call ended. But it was enough.

When Shiffon heard Cora's voice on the other end of the phone saying those magic words she was ecstatic. Now she only had to get in position, wait for the sun to go down and make her move.

Shiffon had been sitting in the parking lot of the apartment complex for hours waiting on Dino. She knew he stopped by here a couple times a week but never did he stay this long. Shiffon began to wonder if it was a mistake choosing this location to make her move. It seemed to be the most ideal because she was hidden in plain sight. Shiffon was able to track Dino without him even being aware.

"My goodness! What is this nigga doing. Let me find out his trifling ass got a chick stashed here. I'm not in the mood for this bullshit," Shiffon complained.

I have to get this shit done tonight. I made a promise to Bailey. Plus the thought of him raping my cousin again makes me sick to my stomach, she thought to herself as she opened her third bag of chips. Shiffon turned up her music and got comfortable. Another hour or so went by and she began dozing off. Luckily the sound of a car alarm going off woke her up.

"Shit!" Shiffon shook her head, to wake herself

up. A few seconds later she saw Dino walking to his truck. "It's time," she said turning on the ignition. She was parked far away but close enough so she could trail him without detection. Shiffon could've pressed the button and blew Dino up right there in the parking lot but she wanted to avoid any unnecessary fatalities. She only wanted one man dead and that was Dino.

Shiffon trailed from a distance as Dino made a right out the apartment complex. It worked in her favor that it was late because there wasn't a lot of traffic on the street. When he pulled up to the first stoplight, she was ready to press play but a car pulled up beside him, so she stopped herself. But then he made a left on a quiet street as if he went the wrong way and was turning around. Shiffon decided it was now or never.

"Bye, bye, Dino." Shiffon's thumb pushed down on the detonator and instantly a fiery eruption with a cloud of fire rose from the ground. It resembled what one might think a gate of hell opening in front of you would be like. The blinding flash followed by a muffled roar and in minutes particles of debris peppering the concrete. Finally it ended with a black turmoil of smoke. "Good riddance you snake ass nigga," Shiffon waved, driving off into the night.

Chapter Fourteen

HOW DID I GET HERE

Picture a hot bubble bath, champagne, surrounded by candles with soothing love music flowing fluidly through the in-ceiling surround sound speakers. That was Bailey's set up. She was celebrating and relishing in her newfound freedom. It had been almost a full week since Dino's demise. With him dead she felt vindicated for his betrayal, lies, deceit but most importantly for breaking her heart. Bailey took a sip of her champagne and a smile spread across her face. Then her ears perked up when the melodic sounds of Case's *Happily Ever After* echoed through the speakers.

"I could've sworn I deleted that from my playlist," Bailey sulked. It was the song she wanted playing on her and Dino's wedding day. Back when she believed they were in love and would be together forever. This nostalgic feeling came over Bailey but it quickly faded away when *Happily Ever After* was replaced with her own voice blaring through the speakers on repeat.

Dino Must Die...Dino Must Die...Dino Must Die...

The champagne glass slipped through Bailey's hand, crashing to the floor. She wanted to leap out the bathtub and make the noise stop but her body was frozen, she couldn't move. She was paralyzed in fear because Bailey knew what this meant. She tried to take deep breaths and calm herself down. She stepped out the tub covered in bubbles, wrapping the plush towel around her wet body. She tiptoed into the entrance of the master bedroom. Nothing seemed out of place but clearly something was very wrong.

Bailey was about to go in Dino's closet and retrieve his gun but remembered it was gone. *Where's my phone,* she thought glancing around the room. *Damn! I left it downstairs in my purse.* There wasn't a landline in the master bedroom, so she had to go downstairs. Bailey decided to unplug a heavy glass lamp from one of the nightstands and use it as a potential weapon. Anxiety consumed her, and it reached an all-time high when the table she always placed her purse on when she first got home, wasn't there. Which meant no car keys, cell phone, no nothing. She raced to the kitchen to retrieve a knife and dial 911 but was stopped in her tracks when Dino appeared like a ghost. Bailey let out an ear piercing scream, swinging the heavy lamp, knocking Dino on the side of his head.

"I'ma kill you, bitch!" He roared, lunging his arm towards Bailey but he grabbed her towel, yanking it off. Bailey's naked body sprinted towards the staircase, hoping to find refuge in one of the bedrooms. Upon reaching the halfway point on the staircase, she felt Dino's strong arm grasping at her leg before his large hand latched on to her ankle. Pulling Bailey back down.

"Let go of me!" She wailed, doing her best to use her other leg to kick Dino's arm and free herself from his grip.

"Nah Bailey! Now it's yo' time to die!"

Shiffon was on her way home when she got the call from Essence. She almost missed it due to how loud her music was turned up. "What's up!"

"Girl, we got a serious problem."

Shiffon decided to turn her music completely off because she wanted to hear every word Essence said, as she rarely sounded distraught.

"What kind of problem we got and you all the way in North Carolina?"

"You know I'm still staying with my homegirl. Well her boyfriend just left here. Guess who reached out to him to see about buying some drugs."

"Can't be. I saw that nigga's car blow up and he was in it." Or so Shiffon thought. She immediately started second guessing herself. "It was dark and I saw him from a distance. I just assumed it was him but he was wearing a baseball cap. Dino always did."

"I don't know who was in that car but it wasn't Dino's ass."

"Maybe it was someone pretending to be Dino who called him." Shiffon wanted to believe.

"Maybe but I seriously doubt it. You must've killed the wrong man. Dino even mentioned to him, he was laying low right now and not to tell anyone they spoke."

Shiffon did recall Bailey mentioning the medical examiner was waiting for Dino's dental records to compare it to the burned body found in the car. They looked at it as simply being protocol to confirm his death, since both were positive he was very much dead.

"Essence, I have to go. I have to warn Bailey!"

"Okay, call me and be careful."

"I'm not worried about me. If Dino found out Bailey had anything to do with the car explosion, she's a dead woman." Shiffon hung up with Essence and started blowing up her cousin's phone. "Bailey pick up! Please pick up Bailey!" She tossed her phone on the passenger seat and quickly did a U-turn.

Bailey's battered and bruised body was tied to the bed post. Instead of just getting it over with and killing her, Dino got more pleasue from making her suffer.

"Wake the fuck up!" Dino smacked Bailey's face. "Open them eyes. I want you to see everythang I do to you!" He taunted.

"Please stop, Dino," Bailey mumbled. She could barely talk. Her body was limp and energy nonexistent.

"Don't beg me now. You shoulda thought this shit through. I knew yo' ass was actin' strange. Too many things won't adding up. Niggas tryna shoot at me the robbery..."

"I told you, I had nothing to do with that shooting," Bailey muttered.

"I know but when bad shit keep happening, it make a nigga paranoid. That's why I put a listening device in the rooms in this house. I felt it had to be somebody close who was able to get to me, and I was right. What they say...these hoes ain't loyal," Dino goaded.

"You should know. Fucking Tori behind my back in our bed. She was supposed to be my best friend and you my man."

"You knew what type of nigga I was, and I told yo' dumbass them broads won't none of yo' friend but you didn't listen. I guess you had to see me fuckin' Tori to finally get it. And my poor nigga Pete had to die cause yo' stupid ass tryna kill me over some pussy," Dino scoffed.

"It wasn't just pussy, Dino. I thought of you and Tori like family. Both of you betrayed me and broke my heart." One tear trickled down Bailey's cheek because she didn't have the strength for a full blown sob session.

"Wait a minute." Dino paused for a second taking in what Bailey said. "Me and Tori broke yo' heart. I don't know why I didn't think of this shit before. It was you that killed Tori wasn't it?"

"No. I didn't kill Tori."

"Stop lyin'!"

"I didn't."

"Just cause you ain't pull the trigger don't mean you didn't kill her. Just like you didn't blow my car up but orchestrated that bullshit."

Bailey was too tired to argue with Dino. At this point she no longer cared. She wanted him to put her out of her misery. Death was inevitable and with the pain she was in right now, Bailey was ready to meet her maker.

"You've already made up your mind. Just kill me and get it over with."

"Not until you tell me what I wanna know." Dino was standing over Bailey. He reached down, wrapping a chunk of her hair around his hand. Grasping it tightly. "Who did you get to put that bomb in my car? Tell me now and I'll put yo' ass to sleep peacefully. I'ma ask you one mo' time. If you make me ask again, I'ma slit you open like a pig," Dino threatened.

"I can't believe I was ever in love with a monster like you," Bailey conceded with bleakness in her voice.

"Stay on topic, Bailey. I wanna name. Who tried to kill me?"

"It was me!" Shiffon announced entering the bedroom. "But this time I won't fuck up."

Dino released Bailey's hair and reached for his gun on the nightstand. But he wasn't swift enough to match Shiffon. She came prepared with a .357 Magnum King Cobra double action revolver with a 3-inch barrel. She emptied the six rounds in Dino's body, guaranteeing he would never make a comeback

"Bailey are you okay?!" Shiffon untied the ropes around her wrist and grabbed the sheet to cover her naked body. "I'ma get you to the hospital."

"I just wanna sleep." Her words were slurred and she could hardly walk. Shiffon had to do her best to carry her cousin out the house. She debated if she should call for an ambulance but Dino had beat Bailey to the brink of death. Shiffon worried her cousin wouldn't make it that long. She stepped over Dino's bullet ridden body, determined to save Bailey's life.

Epilogue

TWO MONTHS LATER...

"I think that's the last box," Shiffon told Essence, looking around the empty house, making sure she didn't miss anything.

"I'm glad we gettin' outta here. It's a beautiful house but between you shooting Dino dead, and poor Bailey almost getting killed here, this house feels haunted," Essence frowned.

"I get it. I can't wait to leave this house. The only reason I came was because I didn't want Bailey to have to come back here. Dino deserved every bullet he got for what he put my cousin through. After all this time, she's just now able to leave the hospital. I hope that nigga burn in hell."

"Yeah, when I first went to the hospital and saw her laying there, I swear I thought I was in the wrong room. I didn't even recognize Bailey."

"I know. It broke my heart seeing her like that. But hopefully she can put Dino and that nightmare behind her."

"I think having her move in with you, will help a lot."

"I think so too," Shiffon agreed. "Physically she's pretty much made a full recovery but emotionally, that will take some time," Shiffon said as her and Essence walked out to the U-Haul truck she rented.

"Are you expecting somebody?" Essence asked when she noticed a silver Range Rover driving up.

"No." Shiffon quickly put the box she was carrying inside the truck. "Are you carrying?"

"No! Are you?"

"Of course." Shiffon hurried to open the front door. She grabbed her purse and pulled out her gun."

"Girl, why you running around in broad daylight wit' a gun?" Essence smacked.

"For times like this. What if that's one of Dino's people in the truck?"

"And?! Don't nobody know you the one who killed Dino. Bailey told the police it was a home invasion gone terribly wrong."

"You never know wit' muthafuckas. Just stand behind me," Shiffon advised as the truck got closer. She positioned her arm ready to fire on sight. The back tinted window slowly rolled down and a nice looking man, who appeared to be in his mid-thirties was staring back at her.

"Are you Shiffon?" he questioned.

"Who wants to know?"

"My name is Alex Flint. Binky gave me your information. He's been trying to call you but umm you didn't answer."

"Oh shit, I left my phone in the truck," Shiffon said, realizing she hadn't checked it in hours.

"He said I might catch you here. Do you have a minute to get in and speak with me?" Alex asked.

"Sure. Essence wait in the truck for me."

"Are you sure and who is Binky?" Essence wanted to know.

"Binky is the guy I told you about...who would get us assassin jobs." Shiffon whispered.

"Oh yeah," she smiled.

"You don't need that." Alex nodded his head towards the gun Shiffon was still holding.

"Almost forgot. Here hold this for me." Shiffon

handed the weapon to her friend before getting in the back of the truck.

"I'll be right here if you need me!" Essence yelled out.

"So what can I do for you, Alex?" Shiffon noticed the burly driver sitting up front. She could feel Alex sizing her up and it made her uncomfortable. They did call themselves Bad Bitches Only but yet she was looking a bit rough and sweaty, after spending hours packing then cleaning out the house. I mean it's not like Shiffon knew she would be meeting a potential client. "Is there a problem?" she popped. Annoyed with the man staring her down but not speaking a word.

"I apologize. I wanted to make sure you're the right fit."

"I know I look a little rough right now," she remarked, glancing down at her old t-shirt and jeans. "But I clean up well."

"I believe you." Alex cracked a half smile. "It's just the job I'm interested in hiring you for, requires you to live up to the name of your company."

"What type of job is it?" the man had piqued Shiffon's interest. Alex opened an envelope on his lap and pulled out a dozen or so pictures of various women. "Okay, so I see a bunch of different women who seem to have very expensive taste," she shrugged.

"Do you remember a couple months ago when Taz Boy was arrested?"

"The rapper. Yeah, it was all over the news. They raided his mansion and found a bunch of drugs and guns."

"It was a set up and one of these women is responsible for that raid. They're working with the Feds."

"These chicks?!" not hiding her shock. Shiffon picked up the pictures again. "The only thing these women look like they interested in raiding is the Louis Vuitton store. When did groupies start working with the Feds?"

"These women aren't groupies. They're clout chasers. They want more than just fuckin' famous men and partying with them. They want fame themselves."

"A'ight, so ambitious groupies. What does that have to do with the Feds?" Shiffon asked.

"Because one of these women are pretending and playing the role of a clout chaser. I need you to find out which one and kill her."

"I see these chicks done pissed you off."

"Only one. Look, if a woman wants to get her come up off a famous man, that's between them. I'm not in the business of stopping someone's hustle. But I'll be damned if I'm going to let someone stop mine. I own the record label Taz Boy is signed to. Between lawyer fees, bail money and all the other bullshit that comes with cleaning up this mess, pissed isn't a strong enough word to describe how I feel. "

"I hear you. So where can I find these women?"

"Does that mean you're taking the job?"

"Are you hiring me for it?"

"Only if you can guarantee me you'll get it done."

"Oh, we'll get it done." Shiffon stated with confidence. "I'm sure Binky provided you with the pricing for our services, including separate fees for expenses."

"Yes he did and I don't have a problem with any of it."

"Good. Because since you want us to infiltrate these clout chasers we must look the part. And like I first said, they appear to have very expensive taste," Shiffon smiled.

"Whatever you need," Alex agreed.

"Then I'm looking forward to doing business with you." Shiffon shook Alex's hand and she officially scored her very first client for Bad Bitches Only.

Coming Soon....

A KING PRODUCTION

Bad Bitches Only

ASSASSINS...

EPISODE 2
(Clout Chasers)

JOY DEJA KING

ORDER FORM

Name:

Address:

City/State:

Zip:

QUANTITY	TITLES	PRICE	TOTAL
	Bitch	$15.00	
	Bitch Reloaded	$15.00	
	The Bitch Is Back	$15.00	
	Queen Bitch	$15.00	
	Last Bitch Standing	$15.00	
	Superstar	$15.00	
	Ride Wit' Me	$12.00	
	Ride Wit' Me Part 2	$15.00	
	Stackin' Paper	$15.00	
	Trife Life To Lavish	$15.00	
	Trife Life To Lavish II	$15.00	
	Stackin' Paper II	$15.00	
	Rich or Famous	$15.00	
	Rich or Famous Part 2	$15.00	
	Rich or Famous Part 3	$15.00	
	Bitch A New Beginning	$15.00	
	Mafia Princess Part 1	$15.00	
	Mafia Princess Part 2	$15.00	
	Mafia Princess Part 3	$15.00	
	Mafia Princess Part 4	$15.00	
	Mafia Princess Part 5	$15.00	
	Boss Bitch	$15.00	
	Baller Bitches Vol. 1	$15.00	
	Baller Bitches Vol. 2	$15.00	
	Baller Bitches Vol. 3	$15.00	
	Bad Bitch	$15.00	
	Still The Baddest Bitch	$15.00	
	Power	$15.00	
	Power Part 2	$15.00	
	Drake	$15.00	
	Drake Part 2	$15.00	
	Female Hustler	$15.00	
	Female Hustler Part 2	$15.00	
	Female Hustler Part 3	$15.00	
	Female Hustler Part 4	$15.00	
	Female Hustler Part 5	$15.00	
	Female Hustler Part 6	$15.00	
	Princess Fever "Birthday Bash"	$9.99	
	Nico Carter The Men Of The Bitch Series	$15.00	
	Bitch The Beginning Of The End	$15.00	
	Supreme...Men Of The Bitch Series	$15.00	
	Bitch The Final Chapter	$15.00	
	Stackin' Paper III	$15.00	
	Men Of The Bitch Series And The Women Who Love Them	$15.00	
	Coke Like The 80s	$15.00	
	Baller Bitches The Reunion Vol. 4	$15.00	
	Stackin' Paper IV	$15.00	
	The Legacy	$15.00	
	Lovin' Thy Enemy	$15.00	
	Stackin' Paper V	$15.00	
	The Legacy Part 2	$15.00	

Shipping/Handling (Via Priority Mail) $7.50 1-2 Books, $15.00 3-4 Books add $1.95 for ea. Additional book.
Total: $_____ FORMS OF ACCEPTED PAYMENTS: Certified or government issued checks and money Orders, all mail in orders take 5-7 Business days to be delivered